KAYLA WREN

Roomies

BLACK CHERRY
PUBLISHING

Contents

Keep in touch with Kayla!

Want to hear about new releases, sales, bonus content and other cool stuff? Sign up for Kayla's newsletter at www.kaylawrena uthor.com/newsletter!

1

Florence

F*ive years earlier*

I snatch a flute of champagne off a passing waiter's tray, wincing and shrugging when the man raises his eyebrow. No, I'm not twenty-one. I'm not even eighteen. But this party is going to be painful enough without trying to get through it on lemonade.

It's not like I'm a big drinker. One glass of bubbly makes my cheeks flush, and I don't like the part where my head starts to spin. So I'm not going to get trashed and ruin the evening—stand down, mister waiter. We're good.

I must pass inspection, because the waiter sniffs and moves on, his tray bobbing as he weaves across the ballroom. I blow out a hard breath and sag back against a pillar, my bare back sticking to the marble. The glass trembles in my hand as I take a sip, sharp sweetness spreading over my tongue, and I scan the room as I swallow—always scanning, scanning.

He's never far from my mind, and he's always the first person I look for.

Adrian.

He promised he'd come tonight. He promised, his green eyes twinkling above his lopsided smile. My heart pounds faster just at the thought of him—my brother's best friend.

My friend, too. No matter what Theo says. Adrian has always been sweet to me, has always talked to me when I hang around them, bored and lonely. Even when Theo tries to shoo me away, rolling his eyes, Adrian is kind. He takes my side.

The conversation around me is a constant hum. There's the clink of glasses; bursts of controlled laughter; the whisper of the breeze rolling in from the gardens, fluttering the white silk drapes. A string quartet play on a raised stage, their lilting melody not quite loud enough to dance to.

It's such a Mom and Dad party. All image and style; a networking opportunity. Nothing to do with Theo. Not really. But my big brother is leaving for college on the other side of the country, and tonight is our last night with him.

With him, and Adrian.

It's so typical. Most of the guests are business partners and local power players. Politicians and actors and investors. Big names and bigger checkbooks, and who are we kidding by saying this party is for Theo? The only people here who give two shits about my brother are Adrian and I. And Adrian only got invited because Theo put his foot down.

"Florence!"

My mother drifts over on a floral-scented breeze. With her sleek red updo and her draping cream gown, she looks like a mythical muse just skipped out of one of the huge oil paintings lining the walls. Her eyes scan me, just like the waiter.

"Oh, darling." She twists her painted mouth sadly. "Are you missing him already?"

Heat crawls up my neck. How tragic do I look, exactly? I fight to keep my expression light, sipping my stolen champagne to buy time.

She doesn't even notice the drink.

"No," I rasp, lowering the glass, "I'll see Theo over break. He's not going to forget us just because he's at college."

"Nonsense." Mom waves a hand airily, giving me what she seems to think is an encouraging smile. "He'll be so busy. Making new friends; building a life. But this is your chance too! It's the perfect time to work on yourself."

Her eyes drop down my body, so quickly I nearly miss it, then she rallies and smiles.

Awesome. Thanks, Mom.

"Have you seen Adrian?" I scan the room over her shoulder. It's a sea of coiffed hairstyles and shining bald heads. No sign of Adrian's dark blond hair, messy and wild.

"Who? Oh, yes of course." Mom hums, turning to scan alongside me. She clicks her tongue gently—a habit she scolds me for—and nudges me with her elbow as we look. "By all means, say hello to him. But don't get your hopes up, darling."

"What is that supposed to mean?" The flush steals over my cheeks, and my palm dampens on the champagne flute. "Adrian's my friend."

Mom gives an uncharacteristic grunt, not deigning to explain herself.

It's impossible that she knows. I haven't told anyone my plan for tonight. Not Theo, and definitely not her. For starters, I don't trust them not to make fun of me. Or even worse, not to pity me.

And second, I like keeping this secret. Tucking it away, warm in my chest.

"There he is!" Too ladylike to point, Mom tips her chin at the open French doors, leading straight into the grounds. One young man there sticks out immediately, his discomfort rolling off him in waves. He leans against a door frame, one hand shoved in his pocket, the other scratching the back of his neck. His borrowed suit strains against his shoulders; a flash of tattoo winks from his wrist.

Adrian.

"Oh, good lord." My mother huffs, shaking her head. "You have giant love hearts in your eyes."

"No I don't."

Her tinkling laugh draws glances. "Of course you do. You always do, darling. Well." She pats her hair. "Must circulate. Try not to be too obvious."

I watch her sashay across the ballroom, irritation and love swirling in my stomach. She means well. And she loves me. She does.

But my mother is hard work.

* * *

"Adrian!" My voice comes out too loud. Kind of strangled. A group of bankers or lawyers or whatever look over, chuckling. I ignore them, marching past with my heels smacking against the floor.

God, my feet hurt already.

I don't care what these people think. And this is why: the relieved smile breaking over Adrian's face. His eyes crinkle at the corners, his mouth tugging up on one side, and the world's prettiest dimple comes out to play. Adrian pushes off the door frame, standing upright, and crushes me to his chest in a one-armed hug.

He always does this. Hugs me. And every time, my insides go crazy. Like someone's picked me up and shaken me upside down, jumbling all my bits together.

"Hi." I beam at him when we break apart. "I'm so glad you're here."

"Are you?" Adrian snorts, turning back to the ballroom. "I'm not. The waiters keep trying to hand me their trays."

I can't tell if he's joking. He gets like this sometimes. Dry and prickly. Teasing that we'll mistake him for the maid.

"Maybe you should take one. Snag us some champagne."

Adrian's smile twitches bigger. "No way. Remember last time?"

I do. God, I always will. This humiliation will be carved into my tombstone. The one and only time I've ever been drunk was last year at Theo's eighteenth birthday party. It was just like this—a crowded room full of rich people who like to talk about the stock market, and the three of us. So bored we were climbing out of our skins.

We grabbed a bottle each. Headed out to the ornamental maze. And I got so drunk, I threw up on Adrian's shoes.

"I don't recall." I ignore his smoky laugh. Focus on breathing slowly. Normally. Like a human.

Is it normal to hyperventilate around your crush? Maybe I should see a doctor.

"Where's Theo?" he asks suddenly, and my heart sinks. Because Adrian's not here for me. Not really. He's here for my brother. And though I tell everyone who will listen that he's my friend too, I have no delusions about which one of us he'd choose.

"With Dad, I think." Adrian grunts, the noise sour. I don't

5

blame him—Dad does not know what to make of Adrian, and the feeling is mutual.

I like to think it's the tattoos, and not that he's poor.

Adrian insists he knows better.

"I'll wait, then." Good to know that we're killing time. *Sorry, heart.* But then he grins at me, and I perk back up again. "Maybe we should go back to the maze."

I scoff. "In these shoes?"

Adrian winces at my battered feet. "Yeah, maybe not. I could carry you?"

I laugh that off, the sound strangled, even as a knot forms in my stomach. Is that another joke? Is he making fun of me? And Adrian frowns at me, bemused. He opens his mouth to say something, but the trill of a spoon against a crystal glass kills the chatter.

The string quartet fades to silence. Everyone turns, expectant, as my father steps onto the dais.

Another speech, then. And he doesn't waste time, launching straight into how proud he is of Theo, how sorely he'll be missed. How his only son is about to make his mark on the world. Theo hovers by the platform, smiling awkwardly at the other guests, a flush creeping over his cheeks the longer Dad goes on. We're a family of redheads, and that means radioactive blushes.

At least Mom and I hide some of it with makeup. Poor Theo.

I turn to Adrian, ready to laugh at my crimson older brother, but the French doors are empty beside me. A cool evening breeze wafts over my bare shoulders, and footsteps crunch over gravel in the garden as someone strides away.

I throw one last glance at my brother. He tips his head back, laughing at something Dad said. Theo's fine—he's more than fine, he's about to start a new chapter in college—and this might be my only chance for my plan.

I need Adrian. Alone. Away from prying eyes and straining ears, so I can finally be honest and set things in motion.

Tonight, I'm going to tell my brother's best friend how I feel.

* * *

The gardens surrounding our mansion are kind of embarrassing. I mentioned it to Mom once, but she hushed me, told me I was being ridiculous. That there's no shame in liking nice things.

But do nice things need so many fountains?

It never bothered me before Adrian. Before Theo dragged home his unlikely new friend, oblivious to Mom and Dad's shared glances. But seeing thirteen year-old Adrian's wide eyes—not dazzled, more dazed—made me see our grounds with fresh eyes.

They're show-off gardens. Look-at-all-our-money gardens. They're meant to make people feel small. And I try not to look at them as I follow Adrian's crunching footsteps, picking my way carefully across the gravel in my heels. The scent of jasmine hangs thick in the evening air, and the sky is bruised pink by the sun set.

A chauffeur lounges against the pale stone wall, sucking hard on a cigarette. He jerks upright when he sees me, but I wave him off, hurrying after Adrian with the long skirt of my olive silk dress clutched in one hand.

I round a corner and see him. He's off the path, striding across the gardens, head ducked low to his chest. I curse under my breath before kicking my heels off. Mom will kill me if she

7

sees me running around barefoot, so I snatch up the evidence before jogging over the springy grass.

I need to talk to him. This might be my only chance.

"Adrian!" I stumble and catch myself, puffing hard as I rush after him. Jeez, does he have to walk so fast? "Slow down! I need to tell you something."

"Go back inside," he yells without turning, his voice hard. My steps slow to a walk, my pulse skittering in my throat.

He's never sounded like that before.

"What's going on?" I call.

"Leave it." He plunges further away, his steps jerky. His shoulders are tensed, bunched up around his shoulders. As I watch, his head twitches to one side, like he's trying to shake something away.

No. No, this isn't… this doesn't make any sense. Adrian is always kind. Calm. He smiles even when he's tired from working two jobs after school.

It must be Dad. He always sets Adrian on edge. Draws that prickliness out even worse. So I set my jaw and push after him, feet pounding over the grass as I try to catch up.

I can handle a bad mood. We're friends. I follow him up the stone steps into a gazebo, wheezing as I toss my heels to the floor. He's pacing, still not looking at me, and irritation crawls up my throat.

So Theo is leaving. I get it; it sucks. Believe me, I'm going to miss my brother more than anyone.

"Go back to the party, Florence." He speaks to the floor, his arms crossed over his chest. His hands are balled into fists by his ribs. "I can't do this right now." Something about the way he's acting—his heaving chest, his clenched jaw, his blank eyes—nudges the back of my mind.

8

I've seen this before, last summer, when one of our maids found a snake under a guest bed. She couldn't catch her breath, couldn't stop scrabbling at the walls.

He's panicking.

"Adrian. What is it?"

"It's nothing. I just want you to *leave*." He rakes a hand through his hair, staring at the gazebo rafters. "You don't fucking listen, do you? Always trailing after us like a kicked puppy. You never take a goddamn hint." His hand shakes as he lowers it, shoving it into his pocket.

Finally, he looks at me, his mouth pressed in a harsh line.

Something flickers behind his eyes.

"Right. Um." I snatch my heels up again, head woozy. "That's—okay. S-sorry."

He waits until I'm on the steps. Until I'm almost away from him. Then he calls out, voice strained.

"Florence. Shit. That's not—wait a second."

I wave a hand without looking.

"No, thank you."

"*Florence.*"

I stumble onto the grass, pulse racing. My heart is pounding so hard it might crack a rib. So hard it makes me feel sick.

Adrian doesn't come after me.

And there's no need.

I got my answer.

2

Florence

resent day

P*resent day*

I swipe an empty champagne flute off a table, holding it up to the light. All around me, the ballroom echoes with the clatter of chairs and the whisper of table cloths as the staff prepare for tonight's charity auction. I squint at the glass in my hand, checking for specks of dust.

Nothing. It's perfect. It's all perfect.

"Relax." Eva, my mother's newest event planner, winks at me as she strides past. Her heels click against the floor, so confident and commanding, her sleek black hair pulled over one shoulder.

Relax. Yeah. I could do that. I could relax.

… After tonight's auction. Once three months of my work have finally come off without a hitch.

For the millionth time today, I wish Theo were here. My goofy big brother, and only ally in this family. He was supposed to be, he swore he'd come when I first planned this event, but the letter I got from him last week didn't even mention the

10

auction.

Gone traveling. Don't tell Mom and Dad! Here's the key to my place in case you need a break from their crazy.

So much for spending more time together after college. Theo's broken free. While I, somehow, got drawn back into my parents' net. Into fundraisers and galas and family obligations.

I didn't even study across the country like Theo. I went to the liberal arts college near here, and somehow I wound up living at home the whole time.

I had my chance to leave. And I didn't take it. There was something about the heartbroken look on my mother's face when I suggested dorms, the guilt trip my father laid on me about extra costs, that made me feel like the world's biggest jerk for even thinking of it.

There'd be time after college—that's what I thought.

I put the glass down with a thump.

"Darling." My mother's voice floats to me across the expanse of tables. They're islands in a sea of marble, draped with pristine white tablecloths, bristling with sparkling cutlery. She gestures from the ballroom entrance. "Come here a moment."

"Uh. Can it wait?" I pick my way between the tables, already knowing her answer.

She scoffs, her pert nose wrinkling. "Of course not. Come along, Florence."

My own feet pad quietly over the marble, and Mom frowns at my ballet flats.

"I'll wear heels later," I tell her before she can complain, joining her in the archway. "These are just for the set up."

"But you don't need to set up." Confusion and despair crease her beautiful forehead. "We pay the staff for that."

"I know." I don't explain any further. Because explaining to

11

my beautiful, distant mother that I need to keep busy, that I want to build skills—I might as well chat to the mirror. "What is it, Mom?"

Her frown smooths away. Like it was never there. Her face is dewy and serene once more, and she claps her hands together. Tucks them under her chin.

"I have a surprise for you."

Dread curls through my stomach.

"What kind of surprise?" I ask weakly, but she's already pinched the sleeve of my blouse and drawn me into the hallway. Two women stand beside a covered dressing rail, one of them holding a clipboard.

They're both sleek—one dark haired and one fair. And they both have the bearing of army generals.

"A makeover!" Mom bursts out, unable to contain herself any longer. "We're going to reinvent you completely. Won't that be fun?"

Uh.

Fun?

"What do you mean, reinvent me?" I eye the dress rail, bristling with dark garment bags.

"Oh, you know. Your clothes. Hair. Your whole *look*. We're going to fill you with confidence, ready to meet some nice young men."

I squeeze my eyes shut, head still turned towards the dress rail. "I'm busy," I grind out. "I'm setting up for the auction."

"Please," Mom scoffs, tittering with her makeover generals. "That's hardly important."

"It's for vaccine research—"

"Yes, but they don't need *you*, do they?"

I turn to my mother at last. She's staring at me, face so

beseeching, her hands spread wide.

And the worst thing is, she's right. They don't need my help. Since finishing college, I've worked flat out on this event. I've lost sleep; fretted about menus; made hundreds of calls.

And do they need me? No, not really. Eva has it covered.

So what *am* I still here for? What is the purpose of my life?

What the hell is the point of all this?

"Florence?" Mom tilts her head. "Are you feeling well? You look queasy."

"Yeah, I…" I clear my throat. "I have to go."

* * *

Packing a bag is a humbling experience. Not because I'm leaving—no, that part feels freaking amazing. Like I'm shrugging off an old musty coat that was only weighing me down. It's humbling because I have no idea what to take.

Which things are important, out in the real world?

I chew on my thumbnail, tossing odds and ends into a designer duffel bag. Underwear. Pajamas. Jeans and sweaters; skirts and dresses. Absolutely no high heels. The clothes and the toothbrush and all that crap—I can figure that out easily enough.

Then comes my passport. My personal documents. I pull my family credit cards from my wallet, staring at them.

Snip. Snip. Snip.

Cutting through those cards… I wince with every slice.

I know I'm forgetting a ton. That I'll kick myself for not planning properly. But now that I've made this decision, I can't get out of here quick enough. This mansion is the only home I've ever known. And at some point along the line, it became a prison.

A fortunate prison. A self-inflicted one.

But a prison nonetheless.

I grunt as I swing my duffel bag onto my shoulder, stumbling forward a half step. My room has been gutted, pulled apart by a righteous tornado, and I look around with smug satisfaction.

I'm wearing my oldest, comfiest sneakers. That feels like a good start.

I snatch up Theo's key. His hurried handwritten letter. Tuck them both safely away in my pockets. And when I march down through the French windows that lead from my suite to the gardens, I don't even shout a goodbye. For starters, no one would hear it. The word would bounce around the endless halls until it faded. And second, because I don't want to argue. I don't want a chance to waver.

I'm going. This is it. It's happening.

I plunge across the grass, free arm swinging, a broad smile spreading over my cheeks.

3

Adrian

I tug Theo's refrigerator open, wincing as the door groans on its hinges. I've only been in this apartment for five days, and I'm already getting a twitch. Every appliance, every surface, every piece of furniture—it's all worth more than I could possibly afford. When Theo sent me a spare key and a note, I can guarantee that he never dreamed I'd take him up on it. He knows I'm never comfortable in his place; that I'm too paranoid that I might damage something and not be able to pay.

Well, *surprise, Theo*. A place to live rent free for a few months while I save up for my own tattoo studio—it's too good to turn down.

Especially since I emptied out my savings for my neighbor's son's medical bills.

Jesus. I can never tell Theo about that. He'd laugh so hard he cried, then insist on refilling my bank account. As easy as watering a house plant, never mind that I scraped and sweated for every last penny of those savings.

No. It's not going to happen. I made that choice and I stand

15

by it. If I can undo it, easy as that, it doesn't mean anything. The rent-free apartment, though…

Yeah, I'll take him up on this. And with any luck, knowing Theo with his scattered world tours, I'll be long gone before he steps back on American soil. He never needs to know that it came to this. That I was desperate.

"Motherfucker." I shake out my hand, hissing, after catching my thumb in a cupboard drawer. For some reason, in this new, fancy environment, it's like I've never made a goddamn sandwich. Every chance I get to smack my elbow or nearly drop a mug—I take it. I'd figure it was some kind of self-sabotage, like I'm somehow trying to get caught out here, but it's always been like this with the Lanes.

Theo. And his little sister Florence. In their glossy, dazzling mansion full of sharp edges and stilted silences.

I can't count how many glass paned French doors I accidentally smudged. How many ornamental flower beds I nearly trampled throwing a ball around with Theo. He never even registered the damage, so used to the staff members cleaning up behind him, but I noticed.

I couldn't erase those moments from my brain.

This, at least, is Theo's place. His parents might pay the bills, but there are no staff members here. Only a cleaning lady that stops by every week, and I already told her to keep her wages and take the days off. That I'll let her know when I'm gone and she needs to come back again. She clucked and fussed over me for that, dusting my shoulders like I'm something else to clean, but she took me up on it.

Smart lady.

I carry my plate and mug through to the open plan living room, careful not to bump into anything. Theo's place is

16

a typical bachelor pad—all sleek lines and stainless steel; monochrome paintings and a glass coffee table. It's soulless, but to Theo's credit, the first day he moved in, he had the rigid black leather sofa switched out for a bright teal fabric one which eats anyone who dares to sit on it.

I love that sofa. Half the nights here, I've fallen asleep on it.

The best part is the view. From the sofa, you can stare at the giant TV screen on the wall, sure. Or you can gaze out at the balcony overlooking the city rooftops, with potted ivy climbing the balcony railings.

That ivy has Florence written all over it. It's understated beauty, an injection of character, and Theo probably hasn't noticed that potted plants are a thing. He's charming, but oblivious. Not aware of his surroundings. He definitely hadn't watered any of the ones here before I arrived.

So she brought it. I'm certain. I sip my coffee, frowning at the delicate white and green leaves, wrapping sensuously around the iron railings.

Yeah. That's Florence, alright.

The key sliding into the lock turns my body to stone. For the space between heartbeats, I sit rigid and horrified, the mug lifted halfway to my lips like a paused cartoon. It's okay that I'm here—I was invited, damn it—and Theo is always happy to see me. But still, I feel caught out. With my metaphorical pants down.

The door handle turns, the soft creak echoing through the apartment, and I jolt back to life. I put my mug down too hard, a dribble of coffee sloshing over the rim and pooling around the coaster. My throat is tight as I launch to my feet, tugging on the hem of my black t-shirt. Trying to come up with something, anything to say that will sound casual. Non-committal. Like a friend who decided on a whim to accept the invitation to crash, not a softhearted idiot who emptied out his savings for his neighbor.

Theo can't know. No one can know.

I have to take care of this myself.

The door swings open, and there's a thump. A muttered curse. And now my heart is twisting for a different reason, because I know that soft voice. Those careful, padding steps. Florence Lane moves through the world like she wishes she were a ghost. No noise, no space taken up.

When I was younger, it weighed on my chest. I wanted to make it better for her. And when I got older, when everything between us shifted and turned cold, it pissed me off. This girl was born to every privilege available, and she's still fragile? Really?

But the Florence who drags a straining duffel bag into the living room is not fragile. She's not careful and quiet. She kicks the door shut with her heel, cursing roundly with words that I didn't think she knew, and tosses the bag onto the floorboards with a bang. When she sees me, she jumps, her palm splaying over her chest, but she doesn't cringe away. Doesn't back down like she used to.

"Adrian." Her voice is flat. Amused, somehow, like she's in on some cosmic joke that I'm not. "Of course you're here. Why wouldn't you be?"

I shift my weight. Shove my hands into my pockets.

"Florence. Theo's not here." My eyes snag on her duffel bag again. That's not the bag of someone dropping around for a quick coffee with her brother.

She rolls her eyes, marching straight past me into the kitchen. Florence bustles around like someone who knows every inch of this place by heart, the process of making coffee a well-choreographed routine. She pulls a mug out of the dishwasher. Gets the right cupboard for coffee on the first try. Bumps the cutlery drawer shut with her hip.

"What are you doing here?" I try again, even though I have a sinking feeling that I already know. Florence shrugs, avoiding my gaze as she stirs her coffee briskly, flecks of liquid landing on the counter.

"Crashing. Theo sent me a key. You know how it is. Sometimes it's good to get away."

Lie. That's not the half of it. She won't even look at me, and besides—if that were all this is, she'd have turned around and left the second she saw me. Florence Lane cannot bear two minutes in my presence.

"Bullshit." Huh. Not my smoothest moment. But she's ruffled me; thrown me off kilter. "Theo said I could stay. I've been here for a week already, Lane."

"And?" She smacks the spoon down on the counter. Turns to face me, cocking her hip.

I take her in. I can't help it. I've always been a sucker for Florence Lane's curves. The girl looks like she belongs in a sculptor's workshop. But her next words jolt me out of my reverie.

"This is my brother's place. Blood runs thicker than water, Griffith."

Low blow. Low fucking blow. And it only dawns on her after she's said it—how careless she's been. Why she shouldn't say shit like that to an ex-foster kid.

"Adrian—" she begins, but I cut her off. I don't even want to acknowledge it.

"The mansion not luxe enough? You can't stay in one of your

19

family properties?" I tilt my head, smiling nastily. "Did they finally run out of pretend jobs for you?"

She sucks in a sharp breath, embarrassment and anger flickering behind her eyes. I've hit a nerve without even trying, and I file that away for future reference. I need all the ammo I can get when it comes to this girl.

"I'm staying." Her voice is hoarse. She swipes up her mug, holding it tight enough that her knuckles turn white, but she doesn't take a sip. She just stares at me, chin raised in challenge. "You've got your own place. You've bragged about your independence enough. Why don't you scuttle back to it?"

Because I gave up my apartment the second I got your brother's offer.

Because this place is my last chance to get my life back on track.

I shrug, face blank. "I like it here. Getting a little taste of luxury." Why won't she drink her damn coffee? I'm getting a dry mouth just watching it hovering by her full lips. "Guess you'll have to learn to share. It'll be good for you. Character building."

She chokes out a laugh, but there's no humor to it. "We can't both stay here. I don't want to spend ten minutes with you."

"Off you go, then." I nod at the door. "Don't forget your bag."

"Adrian." She says my name low. It's a plea. "Stop messing with me and leave."

That's what am I to her. What I've always been. A curiosity at first, a fascination, then eventually a non stop pain in her ass. I don't have to try. I just have to exist. And she's always been able to dismiss me like one of her family's staff.

Not here. Not now. I have just as much right to be here. The damn key is digging into my thigh through my jeans pocket. If Theo offered the place to both of us, that's on him. He probably thought neither of us would go for it, but here we are.

And I'm not leaving. Not this time.

I'm desperate.

"Wipe that up when you're done." I nod at the flecks of coffee on the counter. "I sent the cleaning lady away."

"You—"

I don't hear what she calls me. I wheel around and stride across the apartment to the balcony, to the fresh summer breeze and the sunlit rooftops and the goddamn ivy.

* * *

It comes to me all at once. A flash of divine inspiration, as I'm eating my long abandoned sandwich hours later. I'm sitting on the balcony at the wrought iron table, telling myself that I'm not hiding from her. I'm just enjoying the view.

Every time I risk venturing back inside, she's still there. Spreading out. Pulling things out of her duffel. Making herself comfortable.

"Shit." I tear off a chunk of crust, chewing angrily. I'm not hungry. My stomach has been churning queasily since she crashed through that door, but I've always hated wasting food. "Shit."

The thing about Florence is that's she's surprisingly stubborn. God knows she doesn't stand up for herself—apart from with me, apparently—but the girl nurses her grudges like she cultivates her house plants. She tends to them. Fusses over them. Coaxes them to grow up big and strong.

I should know.

Hinting won't make her leave. Not even stating it outright. She won't go, not while she's determined to stick it out. Not

21

while this apartment is a good place to be.

I get it. Her parents are kind of insane, in that unhinged, rich people way. I wouldn't last a week in that mansion. But the Lanes are loaded, and I've seen the family credit cards lining Florence's wallet first hand. She could go anywhere. A hotel, a spa, another country.

She could pull a Theo and disappear off around the world.

So—I can't change her mind. But I can change the context.

I can make this apartment hell, too.

4

Florence

Adrian hasn't been warm for years. Not since Theo's college leaving party. But over time, on the rare occasions we still had to see each other, we settled into a frosty distance.

No need to speak to each other. Definitely no need to hang out. All those times when I was growing up, when I kidded myself that Adrian actually wanted me around—that delusion is long gone.

Now, we're stuck. In a one-bed apartment. It's spacious, sure, but it's also open plan, which means the bedroom and the bathroom are the only way to escape each other's eye lines. Adrian spends most of the afternoon on the balcony, scowling out at the rooftops like they're responsible for this somehow. And I bustle around Theo's apartment, trying to make myself aggressively at home.

When Adrian finally steps back inside, squeezing his shoulders through the glass doorway, he grimaces at my belongings spread over the apartment.

My cell phone is plugged in to charge on the kitchen counter.

My bullet journal and favorite pen rest on the coffee table. There's a soft cream sweater that I don't need to wear right now, but that I draped over the arm of the sofa to make a point.

I rest my elbow on the breakfast bar, smiling at him with dead eyes.

"You're staying, then."

From the way he says it, you'd think I'd sentenced him to life in prison.

"Yep. You know me. I can never take a hint."

His frown deepens. He shoves his hands in his jeans pockets, his shoulders bunching up around his ears. With the evening sun washing over his tan skin and dark blond hair from behind, he's lit up gold.

This is how I used to see him. Borderline angelic. So handsome, he made my lungs seize.

Too bad he's a jackass.

"There's only one bed." His cheeks flush as soon as the words are out. He hurries to keep talking, like I might think he's flirting. God freaking forbid. "I'm not giving up the bedroom. You won't be here long anyway."

"That's fine." I smack a palm against the counter, hopping down off the stool. I turn to face him square on, my legs braced. "I'll take the sofa. It's super comfortable. I helped Theo pick it out."

For some reason, that pisses him off. He jerks his head to the side, muttering under his breath, then stomps to the bedroom without another word. The door slams behind him, the sound bouncing off the walls, and I snort.

Jeez. Outlasting this guy will be child's play. He's so touchy, I've pissed him off without even trying.

And I will try. Adrian might be on some kind of luxurious

24

vacation from life, but since ten o'clock this morning, this *is* my life. I'm cut off. It's self inflicted, but the fall out is still the same. If I leave this apartment, I've got nowhere else to go.

So he can grump and stomp around in those boots all he likes. He can make me sleep on the sofa—hell, he can force me onto the floor.

I'm not leaving. And I won't have to.

He's so easy to piss off, he'll be gone within the hour.

* * *

The scent of roasted garlic makes my stomach clench, growling noisily. Have I eaten today? I hang off the end of the sofa, peering into the kitchen. My bullet journal and pen lay abandoned in my lap, swirled into my nest of blankets.

Doesn't matter. I got as far as uncapping the pen. Writing 'To Do'. Then I got lightheaded.

There's so freaking much to do. So much to think about now I've tossed myself out into the big wide world. And I cheerfully ignore it all as the clanging of pots and pans floats out of the kitchen. Adrian moves around the space with his back turned to me.

There's a dish cloth tossed over his broad shoulder. A tattoo spilling out of his black t-shirt, winding around his arm. I chew on the inside of my cheek, watching him work at the counter. His shoulder blades flex as he slices something.

"What are you making?"

He ignores me. Standard procedure. I crane my neck further, almost toppling onto the rug.

Adrian's jeans have that soft, worn kind of denim. Washed into submission. They cling to the tight swell of his ass; his

25

well muscled thighs. Years ago, I'd have been so jealous of those jeans, I could cry.

Tonight, I tear my eyes away and yell louder.

"Griffith! What are you cooking?"

He twitches his head toward me. Not turning all the way around; just showing the smirk tugging his mouth.

"I'm making dinner."

"Which is?"

"Pasta for one."

I flop back against the cushions, my stomach growling so hard it hurts. Food. Cooking. Being a functional human.

God help me.

No, you know what? I've got this. I shove off the sofa, marching to the kitchen, fully intending to fix myself something fuck-you-delicious. I can't help but slow down when I pass Adrian's pot, though. A rich tomato sauce simmers, glossy and perfect, laced with red wine and garlic.

"Would you like some?" he asks lightly. It's a trap. A freaking trap.

I swallow hard. "No, thank you."

"Suit yourself." He smirks as he stirs the pot. As if he'd ever give up his dinner for me. I glare at him, nostrils flaring, but my stomach chooses this moment to roar its disapproval. And Adrian tips his head back and laughs, the sound as golden as his hair in the sunshine, like it's the funniest thing he's ever heard.

"Shut up." I march past and yank a cupboard open.

Cereal. Okay, that's… an option. I steal a glance at Adrian's pasta sauce, then turn back to my tragic cupboard. Peanut butter. Jelly. Some kind of baking mix. Tins of beans and a sagging packet of lentils.

"Are you sure?"

"Shut. Up."

He chuckles to himself, placing a single plate and fork on the counter. He dishes up quickly, piling spaghetti high then pouring every last drop of sauce over.

He winks at me as he pulls a block of cheese from the refrigerator. Grates it over his food with his muscles flexing and his grin smug.

"God, I hate you."

"Likewise, Lane."

He puts the cheese back and swaggers out of the kitchen. The delicious scent goes with him, leaving only the faint memories behind. I bury my head in the cupboard, head pounding, and force myself to daydream about peanut butter and jelly sandwiches.

Sweet and salty. Soft, pillowy bread.

Come on, you stupid stomach.

It rumbles again on cue, loud and insistent, and I smirk as I set the jars on the counter. Screw Adrian and his plate of wonders.

It was probably gross anyway.

* * *

The sofa is... not as comfortable as I claimed. It's perfect to sit on, to curl up and watch movies and slowly sink into its squashy embrace. But for sleeping?

It sucks. My spine feels like a limp noodle.

"Damn it." I huff loudly and roll over for the fifth time in the last minute, smacking the pillow into shape. The apartment is ghostly quiet, the only lights washing in from the city's aura outside and the red pinpricks of electronics. I've almost settled into sleep a handful of times already, but it keeps dancing out of reach.

As soon as my eyes close and my breathing starts to calm, I feel it. The panic. It climbs up my throat. Squeezes my ribs. And whispers in my ear: *what the hell have I done?* Everything I've left behind lands like a grand piano on my chest. All that security.

Mom and Dad.

I push my face into the pillow and force myself to replay this morning. What living there really means.

Adrian's right. All those times he's lectured Theo about independence, trying to explain why he doesn't want his help—he was right. I always thought he was so annoying, so high and mighty, never mind that he was making everything so much needlessly harder for himself.

But here he is, cooking amazing food. With a job to go to tomorrow.

And here I am, with an overwhelming To Do list that I can't even bring myself to write.

I inhale slowly through my nose, hold it for the count of ten, then let it all go. I'll figure it out. I will. And I won't let Adrian Griffith scare me back to my parents' mansion. Something pinches in my chest at the thought of them, a bruised kernel of homesickness, but I keep breathing. Push it away.

I can't think about that right now. One meltdown at a time.

"Alright, cut it out." The bedroom door bangs open. Adrian stands with his arms crossed in the doorway, his hair mussed but his green eyes bright. The moonlight washes out most colors in the room, but those eyes... I blink. Look away.

"What have I done now?" I address my question to the wall beside him. It's safer. And I don't bother to sit up, staying

28

cocooned in my blankets.

For starters, I don't want to be polite. He doesn't deserve it. And second, I'm wearing the first set of pajamas I grabbed from my bedroom. Little pinstriped satin shorts and a button up shirt.

Something tells me, if Adrian Griffith sees these shorts, he will choke on his tongue. And not in a good way.

"You're huffing. Sighing like I cast you out here like a dog."

"Didn't you?" I tug aimlessly at a loose thread on my pillow.

"Florence. The sofa is fine. Stop being an ass."

That makes me sit up. I lunge upright, my red hair tumbling over my shoulder.

"I'm not being an ass, you troll. I'm trying to sleep. You're the one bursting in here because I breathed too loudly."

"I heard you through the fucking wall!"

"Stop listening then, you creep!"

We break off, chests heaving, scowling at each other. It's an impasse. Another vicious, unresolved spat in a chain of many. I open my mouth, ready to go for round two, but Adrian curses darkly and plunges back into the bedroom. *Goodnight, asshole.* I roll my eyes, shifting to lie down again, but then he strides back out with a pillow tucked one arm.

"Leave the blanket," he says shortly. He comes to stop beside the sofa. So close, I could reach out and graze his stomach with my fingertips.

And what a stomach. It's ridged with muscle, his gray sweatpants hanging low on his hips. The triumph of getting the bedroom fades as quickly as it came.

"Turn around."

He pulls a face. "What?"

"Turn around. I don't want you to see my pajamas."

29

"Why—" he begins to ask, then cuts himself off, shaking his head. He turns quickly, staring out at the balcony. I untangle myself from my blankets, cheeks flushing when my foot gets caught and it takes way too long, then slide off the sofa in a whisper of fabric.

"Listen, Adrian." I snatch my pillow up. "Whatever you do, don't breathe too loudly. It's freaking annoying."

He hisses through his teeth, turning, but I dance across the shadowed living room and into the bedroom before he can reply.

Door closed, I flop down, arms spread onto the mattress. It's firm. So beautifully firm.

That soft hearted idiot. I grin as I crawl up the bed, scrambling under the covers.

He doesn't stand a chance.

5

Adrian

Jax grunts from behind the front desk when I push into the studio. Rocksteady Tattoo Parlor is about what you'd expect from this end of town—bleary glass windows and cases of neon half-plastic piercings. A fluorescent light hangs in reception, its belly full of dead flies, and the smell of microwave popcorn floats in from the staff room.

"You're early." Jax scratches his salt and pepper beard, squinting at the computer monitor. Like I'm not early every day. His wiry chest hairs poke through the gaps between shirt buttons, and there's a cigarette tucked behind his ear.

"Traffic was good."

Lies. I sold my bike for those medical bills. I walked here this morning, the trip taking me over an hour, my backpack chafing against my collarbone.

Jax sucks on his teeth, clicking through today's appointments. "You've got a belly button piercing. Another hour on Mick's back piece. Then you're on walk ins this afternoon. And some girl wants you to cover up her ex boyfriend's name."

My turn to grunt. I'm grateful for this job. I am. And though it's not glamorous, Rocksteady is what's turning my life around. Giving me the skills to open my own studio.

But covering up exes' names is just depressing. I rub my sore shoulder, walking past to the staff room.

"Want a coffee?"

Jax grunts. That means yes. I swipe two mugs out of the cupboard, washing them up again for good measure. Everything in the studio itself is clean. Up to standard. But out in the staff room... all bets are off. As I fish the milk out of the minifridge, I remember Florence stirring her coffee. Flecking hot liquid over the counter.

Then her sighs last night, well past midnight. Her pained huffs, her exhausted groans. I clenched my teeth so hard my gums hurt, listening to her. The woman is a menace.

And those pajamas. That flash of cream pinstriped satin as I turned.

I rub my chest, stirring in Jax's three sugars.

I've got ten minutes before we open. Ten minutes to down my coffee and set up my work station. I dial Theo, putting my phone on speaker and resting it on the stainless steel cart in the studio. Jax slurps his coffee loudly from reception, fiddling with the radio until it blares crackly old rock songs.

"Hey, man." Theo always sounds so damn pleased to hear from me. So bright and warm. It used to freak me out, and I waited for years for that to fade, but it never did. "How's it going? You're up early."

"Why does everyone say that?" I scowl down at the black leather bed, placing a blue paper cover over the top. "I'm always up early. It's you fuckers who sleep in."

"True." There's no shame in his voice. Just amusement. "But I'm mending my ways."

32

I snort. I can't help it. Theo has dozens of good qualities, but he has not exactly had a rough time of it. He could go his whole life without working a single day if he wanted. Just live off that nice fat trust fund.

"I'm serious." Now he sounds defensive. "I swear, Adrian. When I come back, I'm getting a job."

"Come back from where?"

Muffled sounds float down the line. I can practically hear him humming, glancing around. Only Theo Lane could take off round the world and not pay attention to where he's going.

"I'm in Amsterdam."

"You sure about that?"

"Shut up." God, he sounds so much like his sister. My stomach flips. "Anyway, I won't be for long. I'm coming back soon."

My hands still over the bed, grip tightening around the disinfectant. "You just left." I'm not ready yet. I need to save up. Get my shit together.

"Yeah, I know. But like I said. I'm changing my ways." He clears his throat, pausing to swig a drink. Probably pristine spring water from a mountain top. "I'll look around here first. For a week or two. Maybe a month. Then head back stateside and do the whole career thing." My shoulders relax as he talks, the tension bleeding away. A week to Theo is a month to a normal person. And Theo's 'month' is god knows how long.

It's fine. I've still got time. So long as I outlast his sister.

"How's Florence?" he asks suddenly, and I freeze again. Jesus Christ, he's giving me a twinge in my neck.

"Why do you ask that? You know we don't get on."

Theo chuckles. "Right. That's why I asked. I figured if you'd seen her, there would have been fireworks."

33

"Well, I haven't seen her." I don't know why I'm lying. The words come out weird, all hoarse, and surely he can hear the bullshit from an ocean away. But Theo hums and moves on, chattering about some gap year hippies he met by the canal, and I tune him out, getting my work stuff together.

I don't know why I called him. Not really. Not when I can't bring myself to tell him about his apartment, or his sister, or anything else that's going on. But Theo Lane is the closest thing I have to family.

I guess I wanted to hear his voice.

"Listen, man. I've gotta go. It's dinner time here."

"Sure." I press my mouth in a line, trying to focus as he tells me his plans. But the main thing I can hear is the raw thump of my heart. Was I always so goddamn lonely? "I'll call you soon."

I'll say this about Theo: he's affectionate. He welcomes every call, always so thrilled that I like him too.

These goddamn Lanes. They'll be the death of me.

"Don't forget the key to my place!" Theo sings just before he hangs up. "If you want to act out Home Alone."

"Bye, Theo."

The call ends, my cracked phone screen winking on then off. I finish the last of set up in silence, the strains of the radio floating through the open door.

A belly button piercing. A back piece. And an ex's name.

I hope Florence knows how lucky she is with those credit cards.

* * *

She's not there when I get back. Theo's apartment is silent. Cool. It's evening already, the skyline bleeding as the sun sets.

34

I kick my boots off with a curse—they rubbed the whole walk back—and pad into the living room. My pillow and blanket are on the sofa from last night, folded and stacked on one side. Florence's duffel bag is missing.

Triumph surges through my veins, even as my gut sinks.

She's gone. I won.

Then I glance over at the kitchen, and choke out a laugh. It's carnage. Like a hurricane struck only here, in a two meter radius.

Pots and pans and dishes are stacked on the counter, listing dangerously to one side. More than could possibly be needed for one meal. What the hell has she done?

I walk closer, wrinkling my nose when the acrid smell of smoke hits me. A pile of washed up dishes sprawl beside the sink, soap bubbles sliding down the china, and steam curls off the water—she was here recently. I glance around again, peering into the corners of the room.

The bedroom door is closed. And I start towards that, before movement on the balcony catches my eye. A shape is curled up on one of the wrought iron chairs, wrapped in my charcoal hoodie. The hood is tugged up, with curls of flaming red hair teased out by the breeze.

Ah.

I change course, sliding the balcony door wider and stepping out. When I see the bowl of cereal in front of her, I can't help it. Laughter bursts out of me, loud and bright.

"Shut. Up."

I'm still chuckling as I drag out the other chair. I drop into it, leaning forward to catch her eye. Florence glowers back at me, sullen and flushed.

"Lane." I force my voice to stay steady. To ask the question slowly, so I can savor every word. "Do you know how to cook?"

She huffs, but there's not just anger there. She's miserable. And that's what reels me in, makes me stop snickering.

"Shut up, of course I do. Everyone knows how to cook."

I shrug one shoulder. "Not everyone."

"What kind of—"

"Some people never learn." I talk over her bluster. "And some people grow up with cooks and nannies and maids. And they have to learn later."

She swallows, hard. There's so much shame etched on her face, I wish I never laughed at all, grudges be damned.

"I don't even know where to begin."

I lift an eyebrow. "Find a YouTube tutorial. It's not rocket science."

"I didn't bring my laptop. And I don't have Theo's wifi password for my phone."

I sigh. "Give it here, then."

She pauses. Stares at me hard before finally slumping back in her chair. She digs in my hoodie pocket before unlocking her phone and slapping it into my palm.

I don't point out my stolen hoodie. It's too much like kicking her when she's down. And the Lanes have always been like that about each other's belongings. Borrowing and trading freely, just waltzing into each other's rooms when we were growing up, snatching up clothes. Gadgets. Whatever.

I used to watch them, bemused. Like they were some kind of nature documentary. It was so alien to me, they might as well have been another species. In foster care, you either guarded it or you lost it. There was no free circulation. No current of shared belongings swirling around.

I should be annoyed about this, too. Florence taking my

hoodie without asking. But honestly, it looks good on her, the dark shade bringing out the copper highlights in her hair and the milky tone to her skin. And she's burrowed down into it, pulling the collar around her chin and tugging the cuffs over her fingers for comfort.

Fuck. I shouldn't like that.

"I'll put the password in your notes too."

"Thank you."

"And you can borrow my laptop if you need." It's ancient, but better than nothing. And what the hell am I doing, making this easier for her? Making her feel at home? I'm supposed to be chasing her away. So I point at her, giving her the smirk I know she hates. "The kitchen is on you, though. I'm not cleaning up your shit."

"I know." She doesn't try to fight me on that like I expect. She just sounds tired. I hand her phone back, perturbed. "I'll do it now, so you can cook." I open my mouth, but she holds up a palm. "Yeah, I know. A meal for one."

She pushes her chair back and goes inside. And I watch her go, the ivy fluttering in the corner of my eye.

6

Adrian

The first time I met Theo Lane, it was like stumbling into someone else's movie. The kid had a driver, for God's sake. He was dressed in what should have been kids clothes, jeans and a comic book t-shirt, but they were all wrong. Finely made and perfectly fitted.

I was kicking a deflated soccer ball at the wall outside the town library, waiting for my foster mom to finish up with errands. And Theo Lane pulled up in that shiny, stretched out car and hopped out of the backseat, waving goodbye to his driver. He hurried toward the library, flicking his hair out of his eyes, and nearly tripped over his feet when I spoke.

"What are you doing here?"

He blinked up at me. Back then, I towered over Theo. He didn't get his growth spurt for another two years.

"Oh. Well." He glanced over me quickly, took in the frayed hems of my jeans. My t-shirt with the gaping neckline. Theo cleared his throat. "It's the library. I'm getting a book."

His voice wobbled. Not because he was scared, exactly, though I definitely freaked him out. I bet the local kids had barely talked to him before. No—he was in that scratchy age just before your voice drops. We both were, though I was doing a better job of forcing my voice level.

"You can't afford books at home?"

He looked at me funny, then a flush crawled up his neck when he figured I was teasing. I stared at that blush, fascinated. I'd never seen anything like it. Like a vicious rash you could call on command.

"Why d'you need to get it from the library?" I pushed him again. "You can buy any book you want." I said it with the confidence of someone used to measuring up people's situations. When you don't have much, when you grow up hungry or wanting, you become an expert in what everyone else has.

The blush flared hotter.

"It's a bad book," he muttered. Confiding in me, like I somehow deserved his trust after grilling him. And I took him in again: his expensive clothes, neatly pressed and not at all mussed. Like a kid who didn't know how to relax. Who had only ever sat ramrod straight his whole life.

A lazy grin spread over my face. "Bad how?"

His eyes screwed shut. He sucked in a sharp breath, like he was in pain.

"There's sex in it."

Alright. I grinned broader, slinging my arm around his neck. He darted a glance up at me, startled but not scared. And let me lead him into the library.

"Let's go find out about this book."

"Theo."

"Huh?"

"My name's Theo. Theodore Lane."

"Of course it is."

He hadn't told me quite everything about that book. But the brave little shit still led me to it, his shoulders tensed and his chin raised. And when he flicked through the pages until he found the scene he wanted, he blew out a quick breath and handed it to me.

"Oh." I frowned as I read, and he shifted from foot to foot. His weight creaking the dusty library floorboards. "Huh. Well, then."

"I told you." He raised his chin in challenge. His eyes were light blue. The kind of ice that can burn.

I shrugged and handed his book back, playing it off cooler than I felt. I'd read plenty of sneaky sex scenes myself, but never between two men. It wasn't all that different, not really. Tab A, Slot B, or whatever.

"Doesn't seem like a bad book to me."

Theo snorted then. So hard his bangs floated up on his forehead. "You check it out, then."

I've never been able to back down from a challenge. It's ingrained in me, drilled for years and years in the foster system.

Stand your ground. Prove your worth.

"Alright." I swiped it from his hand before he could say anything. Marched to the check out desk and slapped it down in front of the librarian.

I had to sign up for a card. Fill out the little forms and shit. That took some of the bluster out of it. But ten minutes later, we stood on the sidewalk outside together, and Theo was grinning back at me as I handed him his book.

"Don't check it in late," I warned him. "Or I'll come after you for the late fee."

"I won't."

He didn't, either. Theo's always been kind of careless, his head stuck firmly in the clouds, but one thing he's never been casual about is other people's money.

Why would he be? The Lanes are richer than God.

I did come after him though. With a firmer soccer ball. I just couldn't get that blush out of my head.

Here was a kid who wore his emotions painted on his skin. Who clearly couldn't lie for shit.

And I didn't trust anyone. It was a good match.

* * *

I sit at the breakfast bar, chewing slowly as I watch the girl on the balcony. She's taken to sitting out there whenever I'm home, trying to get as far from me as possible without chucking herself over the railings.

She could retreat to her bedroom. She's the only one of us with that option now. But Florence is a Lane through and through. It won't even have occurred to her.

"How's it going?" I call out to her, just to see the pissed off twitch of her head. Her red hair is tangled and wavy, tied up in a messy topknot, and she throws me a scathing look before turning back to my laptop screen. A half-empty mug of coffee rests on the table beside her, forgotten twenty minutes ago.

Just as well. Florence can't brew coffee for shit.

"What are you doing on there?" I call again. She flaps a hand at me, not even looking up.

Briefly, I mull over checking my browser history. What are the chances a girl like Florence knows how to scrub her tracks? But I dismiss the idea as quickly as it came.

More fun to tease it out of her.

41

I scoop my own mug off the breakfast bar, sipping the hot coffee before wandering slowly to the balcony. Over the last three days, I've honed this part. Approaching Florence Lane at the perfect pace to throw her off. Too fast, and she jumps. Slams the laptop shut, pulse pounding in her throat. And if I dawdle too much, she has time to brace herself. Gather her confidence.

"What on earth are you doing on my laptop, Lane?"

She scowls at me where I lean in the doorway. Her eyes flick quickly down my body, then away.

"You said I could borrow it."

"I did."

"So why do you care?"

I shrug one shoulder. "If you're catfishing some poor man, I'd like to be aware."

It's my day off. Mid morning on a sunshine-drenched day. Every atom of me screams to leave this goddamn apartment, to go get some space, to live my life. But I can't resist needling her. Can't help prodding her until she blushes, just like Theo.

Besides. I've been dying to know what she does all day when I'm in the studio.

"This can't be better than Mommy and Daddy's mansion." I fold my arms, dipping my chin. "Why are you here, Lane?"

It's her turn to shrug. To give an airy sigh.

"I told you. I'm taking a break."

"Yeah, all those galas and shopping trips must get exhausting."

She doesn't grace that with an answer. Just keeps scrolling on my laptop, a tiny crease puckering her forehead, and Jesus Christ, what the hell is she doing on there? I'm hovering too much now, losing ground, but I can't help it. I need to know.

"Here." I place my coffee mug down by her elbow. She blinks

42

down at it, confused. And I take the momentary distraction to dart around behind her, crouching and reading over her shoulder.

"A job site?"

She slams the laptop shut, juddering the table. A wave of coffee sloshes over the rim. I pluck up my sacrificial drink, watching her closely over the rim.

Yeah, there's the blush.

Florence Lane is job hunting?

"Daddy can't get you an internship?" I ask lightly. Because suddenly everything I thought I knew about the last few days has been tossed in the air. "That's terrible. I'm so sorry, Lane."

"Shut up."

Except those weren't internships. They weren't the glamorous PR roles and event planning nonsense that a girl like Florence might dabble in.

They were local listings. For waitresses and receptionists.

"Florence Lane." She braces herself before she looks up. Her eyes flutter closed briefly, then she raises her chin and stares at me face on. "Are you playing at being poor?"

She pauses before answering. Her lips part slightly, the breeze tugging a stray red curl against her cheek, and I shove my free hand in my pocket to keep from tucking it behind her ear.

"Adrian?"

I grunt. This is going to be good. And Florence does not disappoint. She folds her hands on the table, neat and prim, and gives me a plastic smile. Her round cheeks lift, so smooth looking. So soft.

"Do me a favor, okay? The next time you want to come and bother me, the next time your single brain cell gets bored—find some other enigma to fixate on. Like how to speak to other humans. Or why your heart shrunk three sizes in the wash. Hey, maybe you could puzzle out how to put the toilet seat down."

She turns back to the laptop, her piece said, and levers it open with a firm set to her jaw. She starts scrolling again, even as I watch, and if it weren't for the red flush creeping up the back of her neck, I'd think she wasn't bothered at all.

I lean down slowly. Until my lips hover an inch beside the delicate shell of her ear.

"You don't fool me, Lane."

I turn inside before I say something more. Something I'd regret.

7

Florence

The phone rings on, pressed against my ear, and I tip my head back and curse at the bathroom ceiling. I pluck at the skirt of my dress as I wait. It's floral and floaty, the perfect dress to start a new life in the city in—and here I am, sprawled on my brother's bathroom tiles.

"Okay." I click the phone off and roll onto my hands and knees. Push to my feet. "Forget the good deed."

I woke up this morning with fire in my belly. Determined to do something right, damn it, to make some progress.

So I made myself breakfast. Oatmeal, from scratch, using a video tutorial like Adrian said.

Then I applied for the first three jobs I found. And decided to tackle cleaning the bathroom.

My fire sputtered out sometime after snaking the shower drain. That was forty minutes ago. And I'd have finished the job, but I can't find a scrubbing brush for the tiles. Theo probably doesn't even have one.

So. Points for effort?

I know what Adrian would say to that, and it pisses me off

45

no end. Because he's right, he's always right about me, and it makes things so much worse.

Well, he won't be right for long. I may be pampered and privileged, unaccountably helpless, but that ends now. Florence Lane is standing on her own two feet.

The sudden buzzing in my palm makes me jump. I stare down at my cell phone, the screen lit up with an unknown number.

No one ever calls me. Even at home, Mom and Dad preferred to send a message with the staff.

"H-hello?"

Any budding hope that this is about a job—it sinks to the tiles when I hear his voice.

Deep. Smooth and melodic, like he belongs hunched over an acoustic guitar.

Adrian.

"Hello, Lane."

"For God's sake." I start to hang up, but his tinny voice floats through the speakers.

"I've got something for you."

I pause. Curse myself. Then press the phone back to my ear. "What?"

He chuckles, dark and smoky. It would be wrong to punch the mirror. Wrong, wrong, wrong.

"Intel." He sounds so freaking pleased with himself.

"What are we, Cold War spies?"

"Things are pretty frosty."

"Adrian."

"Relax." I clench the phone so tight the plastic creaks. "Just thought you should know there's a place hiring here. The dance studio next door."

"I can't dance," I say flatly. It's a lie, actually. My mother made me take ballroom lessons for years, but there's no force in the world that would make me admit it to this man.

He really laughs then. I can picture it exactly: his head tossed back, his eyes crinkling at the corners.

"They're not hiring dancers, you idiot. They're hiring for the front desk."

A receptionist. I could do that.

Answering phones, booking lessons... receiving people? Whatever. I can do it.

"What's the address?"

He rattles it off. I hurry out into the living room and find a notepad, then make him repeat it.

"Anything I should know?"

He snorts. "Like what, exactly?"

"Forget it." The next words are gritted between my teeth. "Thank you."

"You're welcome." Adrian doesn't say it to be polite. He says it to drive his advantage home. To make me feel three inches tall.

Well, joke's on him. I hang up and clatter into the bedroom, pulling clothes out of my duffel.

I've tried applying online. Sending a million emails.

I'm going down there. And I'm getting that job.

* * *

The tattoo parlor where Adrian works is in a rough part of town. The streets are potholed, the stoops lined with empty bottles, and grafitti is sprayed over the brick walls. Even the bus shelter lists to one side, and the scent of kebab meat floats

47

on the air.

There's something beautiful about it too, though. In a harsh sort of way. The sun lights up the glass windows of all the hair salons and nail studios, and those kebabs smell pretty freaking good. My stomach growls as I lock up my car, crossing the street to the Rocksteady Tattoo Parlor. Its black sign juts out into the street, as cocky as its employees.

I've never seen where Adrian works. By the time he started here, things had gone cold between us. We avoided each other like bad smells.

I lean in the window and squint at the front desk. But it's not Adrian—it's some older guy, scratching his chin. He catches me staring, raises a thick eyebrow, so I wave awkwardly and dart away.

This is what I'm here for, anyway, not Adrian: Wonderland Dance House. The sign above the entrance is pale blue with cream lettering, faded in places but still pretty. And the windows are sparkling clean.

When I packed up my bag and fled my parents' mansion, I wasn't really thinking straight. I grabbed odds and ends, random pieces of clothing—definitely no proper outfits. But I did my best back at the apartment, hunting down Theo's ironing board and doing up my hair. Slicking a dusky pink lipstick over my mouth.

My reflection moves in the glass, and I take a steadying breath. I don't look half bad. My black leggings tuck into ankle boots; my purple tunic dress fits me properly for once.

I set back my shoulders and push through the door.

"Hi, love!" A woman in her early forties calls from the front desk. I check over my shoulder for someone coming in behind me, but no. She means me. The woman is a whirlwind of

48

energy, tapping away at her computer, bustling between the shelves behind the desk, tapping her cracked ballpoint pen against her rouged lips.

"Yes—hi. Um. Hello." I twist my fingers together in front of my stomach, then force myself to drop my hands. I've watched so many videos over the last few days. How to Rock a Job Interview. How to Project Confidence. How to Impress a Stranger.

None of them said 'stutter and wring your hands together.'

"I heard you might be hiring." My voice comes out clearer now. Stronger. The woman glances over, her gaze sweeping me behind her thick framed glasses.

"You heard right. You ever worked a front desk?"

"No." I swallow hard and push on. "But I've helped to plan several events. And I have a Business degree from—"

"Alright." She waves a hand, turning back to her computer. "Don't need a degree for this."

She types quickly on her keyboard, her fingers a furious blur. She's not talking to me anymore, not looking at me. Not even acknowledging I exist. I peer back at the doorway—is this done? Am I dismissed? But the thought of my dwindling bank account makes me plant my feet.

It's not over until she says the word 'no'. So I clear my throat and approach the front desk.

"I'm a fast learner. And I'll work hard. Anything you want me to do—cleaning toilets, taking out the trash—I can do it." She glances over at me again, still typing, but her gaze is a tiny bit warmer this time.

"We have some fancy ladies like you in the classes." I don't know what to say to that, so I stay quiet. "Sometimes they don't like to do something. So they refuse. Get all uppity about it."

"I won't, I swear." I draw a cross over my heart, and that makes her mouth twitch up at the corner. I take a deep breath and go for broke. "I really need this job."

The woman grunts. She finally stops typing. She turns to me, one hand propped on her hip.

"You'll need training." It's not a question, but I nod. "It's time consuming, training someone from scratch."

"How long does the training take?"

She wobbles her head, her black topknot sliding left and right. "To start with? A day. A full shift."

"Then let me do a trial." I clasp my hands together to keep from fiddling. "A day's training. And if you still don't want me, I'll go."

She scoffs. "Of course you would go. What are you going to do, camp out?"

Maybe. I'm pretty freaking desperate. But it doesn't come to that.

"Alright." She reaches under the desk and slaps a wrinkled sky blue polo shirt onto the wood. "You're on."

* * *

Jesus Christ, a full day's work is hard. I knew that, from helping out with events. I knew how your feet can throb, hot and achy with every step, and how your back can scream out for you to sit down. But with the events, there were always chances to grab five minutes. To catch my breath and rest my heels.

There are no breaks at Wonderland. The boss, Cindy, ducks out for five minutes now and then to suck down a cigarette in the back alley. But then she's back straight after, working non stop like a maniac. I can't tell if she's stressed or if this is her default setting.

She's blunt. She doesn't mince her words. And when I mess up, she clicks her tongue in a way that makes me cringe.

But she shows me everything, too. Takes the time to walk me through the procedures: how to answer the phone, how to use the online booking systems, all the cleaning check forms and other paperwork.

"There's a lot to it," I murmur partway through the afternoon. I'm wilting over the desk—I've only had a bowl of oatmeal today. My throat is raspy and dry from lack of water.

"You'll get used to it." Cindy winks at me, and I perk up.

I've done it. This is happening.

I still don't take it for granted. This isn't like those jobs that my friends from college got. Jobs with contracts and paperwork and one month's notice.

It's clear: if Cindy doesn't like the way I work, I'm out the door.

That's fine. I'll work so hard, she'll never want me gone.

"Some of the other girls who work here take classes on the side. It's the only freebie you'll get from me, so don't go asking for other favors."

I hadn't planned on it. Didn't even think I'd get classes. But now I click open the timetable, eyeing the names.

Flamenco.

Classical Ballet.

Tango.

Lindy Hop.

"You ever dance?"

"My mom made me take ballroom," I murmur, paging through the week's classes.

Cindy snorts. "I bet she did. Well, there are ballroom classes on Tuesdays and Thursdays, so when you don't have a shift—"

"I always hated ballroom, actually."

Cindy draws herself up to her full height, the top of her head level with my eyes.

"I teach ballroom."

"Oh." My stomach sinks. "Um. Well, I'm sure if you were the one teaching it—"

She tips her head back and roars with laughter. I actually see the metal fillings in her teeth.

"I'm just messing with you. Yeah, ballroom's a drag." She pokes a finger at the screen, her nail glossy with black nail polish. "That's the class for you."

I peer at the word half-obscured by her nail.

Burlesque.

Heat crawls up my neck. Suddenly I feel too big, too flushed, too clumsy.

"Maybe," I manage at last. "I'll think about it. Thank you."

Cindy opens her mouth like she's going to prod at me again. But then the phone rings, the bright chirrup cutting through the quiet, and she's all business again. Back in her non-stop flurry of work.

She doesn't mention it again. And when she finally waves me back into the street, her voice is ten degrees warmer than it was this morning.

"Eight thirty tomorrow morning. Don't be late."

"I won't."

I step outside, let the door swing shut, then hiss and punch the air.

"She can still see you." The low voice floats down the sidewalk. "Glass is see-through, Lane."

I turn to Adrian and shrug, my mouth stretched in a cartoonish grin. I can't help it. The sun is setting, painting the street pink, and my limbs are aching with a whole day's work.

I did it. I actually did it.

"You're looking at the new front desk girl." I drop into a little curtsy, even though he didn't ask. But Adrian gives a crooked smile, walking closer with his hands in his pockets, and for a breathless moment, it's like before. How we were before Theo's leaving party.

"Congratulations." His voice doesn't have the usual mocking edge. And he looks so good in the buttery evening light, his skin warm and his hair glinting gold, that I throw my arms around his neck and squeeze him into a hug.

"Thanks, Griffith." I step back quickly, remembering myself. The telltale heat of a blush creeps up my chest.

"No problem." He falls into step beside me easily as I wander down the sidewalk. Cross the street toward my car. It's not until my hand is on the driver's door that something nudges at my brain. I squint at Adrian where he's rounded to the passenger side.

"What about your bike?"

The smile slides off his face. Just like that, he shuts down.

"Right. Yeah." He steps back, hands shoved in his pockets.

"You can come with me if you want, I just thought—"

"No, you're right. I need to bring my bike."

"Adrian—"

"See you later, Lane." He turns and strides back toward Rocksteady. I glance around the street, but I don't see a motorbike. Only parked cars and chained up push-bikes. I watch Adrian's broad shoulders until he reaches a side road. Disappears down an alley.

Right. That makes sense.

I shake my head, tugging my car door open and sliding into the seat.

No point dwelling on Adrian Griffith. He doesn't like me anyway.

8

Florence

"I don't understand what you're trying to achieve here, darling. You've punished Daddy and I enough. You've made your point: the makeover was wrong. Now come home."

I roll my eyes at the phone resting on the coffee table. I put Mom on speaker as soon as she called. I knew I'd need my hands free to choke the air. Plus, this way I can paint my toenails as we talk. The gentle slide of emerald green polish over my nails—it's soothing.

"I was always going to leave at some point, Mom."

She huffs. "Do you *want* us to worry?"

I glance at the front door, but it stays mercifully shut. There's no way I want Adrian to hear this.

Where the hell did he go after work? He should have been right behind me. If anything, he should have gotten home first, since I drive like a little old lady.

"Nope. But I don't want to live with my parents forever either."

She sighs, scathing. "And where will you live? How will you

pay for food? You really haven't thought through this little rebellion, darling. It costs money to live out there in the world. Money that, since your ridiculous stunt with those credit cards, you no longer have access to." Her tones changes. Softens. Turns coaxing. "We ordered replacements, sweetheart. You can have them when you come home—no hard feelings. Okay?"

"That's kind, Mom." I rub my forehead with my wrist, back and forth, like I can erase the headache brewing under my skull. "And I'm grateful. Truly. But I need to do this. I need to learn to stand on my own, you know?"

"No," she huffs. "I do *not* know."

And I guess she doesn't. She married my father straight out of college. The closest my mom has come to a job is bossing around the mansion's staff. That, and her early acting days.

Does she ever miss it?

Does she ever think about what could have been?

"You let Theo move out," I say quietly. "You didn't give him a hard time." I dab the nail polish brush against the bottle, wiping off a glossy emerald bead. The chemical smell is strong. It burns my nose, and I make a mental note to open the balcony doors before Adrian gets home.

If he ever gets home.

"That's different."

"Why?"

For a moment, I think she's going to answer. That she's actually going to think about my question. She pauses, her breath stilling down the phone. Then she tinkles out a laugh, and the moment's over.

"You know why, darling. It's different for young men. Everything is. Separate rules apply."

"Gross." I switch feet, propping my second heel on the edge

56

of the coffee table. "That's so old fashioned. I thought you hated things that age you."

She sucks in a sharp breath. "Florence!"

I smirk at my wiggling big toe. "Bye, Mom. Love you." I reach over and tap the screen, ending the call before she can work herself into a fury.

It's petty. A mean little victory.

Still feels pretty good.

* * *

Adrian's key slides into the lock over an hour since I left him on the sidewalk outside Rocksteady. He nudges the door open with his shoulder, sighing heavily as he trudges into the living room.

His broad shoulders are slumped under his jacket. Dark shadows bruise his eyes.

He looks exhausted. I gnaw on my bottom lip, watching him kick his boots off and walk to the kitchen. He's moving stiffly, gingerly, and he doesn't even look at me until he's filled a glass of water and leaned against the counter.

"What," he says, raising an eyebrow over the rim. Just like that: *what*. A statement, not a question.

"Where have you been?" I screw the cap back onto the nail polish and set it on the coffee table. He rolls his eyes.

"Who are you, my mother?"

"No, but as your roommate—"

He snorts. "We're not roomies, Lane. We're not even friends."

I clamp my mouth shut. And absolutely refuse to look at the thank you gift I stood on the coffee table.

Thank you gifts are for nice people.

57

Adrian Griffith is a grade A jerk.

"What's with the wine?"

Heat floods my cheeks. I scowl at his stupid cocky grin.

"It's nothing."

"Celebrating your new job?"

"No, I—" I break off, glaring at the bargain bottle. The one I picked out because I know he prefers red. "Yep. That's it."

What was I thinking? I must have had some kind of stroke on the way home, pulling into that store to pick up a gift.

It's just so easy sometimes, to forget what he's really like. That Adrian's a cold-hearted asshole, and not the sweet, steady older guy that I used to idolize him as.

"Lane." Yeah, he's definitely not that guy. His tone is so mocking, I cringe and slide an inch down the sofa. "Admit it. Did you buy that for me?"

"Sure," I say flatly. "The arsenic, too."

I'm ready to snatch it up and drown my sorrows in Theo's bedroom, dignity be damned, but Adrian strides back into the living room before I can move. He plucks the bottle off the coffee table, scanning the label and throwing me a wink.

"Two years old. Wonderful vintage."

"Shut up." I reach for it but he darts away. He swipes two glasses from the kitchen and goes straight to the balcony.

"Are you coming?" Cool night air rolls in as he pushes the door open. The sounds of the street grow louder—distant shouts and car horns, but also the shiver of trees. Faint strains of piano music.

"Screw it." I push to my feet. This may be a terrible idea; I may be throwing myself to the lions.

But I got a job today, damn it.

I deserve some crappy wine.

* * *

There's something about balconies. Something otherworldly. Perching high above the people below, hearing snatches of their conversations, catching whiffs of their dinners cooking. It's like we're gods in Olympus, overseeing the mortals, playing chess to determine their fate.

Wow. I have definitely had enough wine.

I place my glass down on the wrought iron table, nudging it away. The crimson dregs swirl in the base, and my head swims a tiny bit as I stare out over the buildings.

So many lit up windows. Silhouettes moving inside. And the blanket of stars spread over the rooftops, winking with passing planes.

"It's crazy out here," I mutter. "Like a whole other world."

"Out here on the balcony? Or away from your parents' mansion?"

Adrian leans back in his chair, swirling his wine in his glass. He's cocky. So sure of himself, he must never have a doubt in his gorgeous head. And why would he, with those jewel-toned tattoos wrapping around his arms, and those knowing green eyes? That soft hair that falls in his eyes?

"Water." I push back my chair. "I need water." Or I'm liable to say something crazy.

Something like: *I miss you.*

Or: *Why do you hate me, anyway?*

Adrian may be cocky, but he startles when I step back onto the balcony with two glasses of cold water. I set one down in front of him without a word.

Probably should have spat in it. I'm no good at this enemies thing.

"What are you going to do with your newfound freedom?" He tips the water glass back, the column of his tanned throat moving as he swallows. "Florence?"

I jump. Shake myself.

"Um. I don't know. I didn't really make a plan."

He grunts. "How long do you think you'll stay out here before you go back?"

Seriously?

"You make me sound like a released criminal. Like I'm going to reoffend and get sent back to prison."

"Pretty good analogy." He smirks into his glass, taking another drink. Is it me, or are his cheeks flushed too? His eyes are bright, like he feels the same electric current buzzing under his skin that I do.

"I'm serious about this." His cheek dimples. "I *am*. I have a job. I'm going to—to do my own thing."

"Only took you twenty two years to get bored of galas." He grins at me, but I'm not laughing.

"It was the canapes." I snatch up my wine glass and drain the last drops. "They were always salmon mousse. Why the hell would someone mousse a salmon?"

He leans back on his chair and laughs, the sound rich and golden. And when he tips forward, the front two legs of his chair thud against the stone.

"Life has been hard on you."

His fingertip traces along my cheekbone. I turn to stone, my heart hammering in my chest. Adrian catches an escaped strand of my hair, one that keeps tugging in the breeze and sticking to the corner of my mouth. He catches it and draws a soft line to my temple, tucking the strand behind my ear.

The moment stretches between us. Taut and shuddering.

"Adrian," I whisper, and he pulls his hand away.

"Rich people will mousse anything," he says, like nothing happened. "Have you seen the fancy cooking shows? They can't eat unless it's foam."

"Right."

He pushes to his feet, squeezing my shoulder before he ducks inside. His hand print burns through my clothes long after he's gone.

9

Adrian

Florence Lane is fucking with me.

Not on purpose. Whatever her many flaws, she's not that cruel. She wouldn't lead a guy on.

But she's smiling at me. Talking to me again, like she used to. Asking questions and waiting to hear the answers. It's a heady feeling—her full attention. I'm like one of her scruffy houseplants unfurling in the sun.

And three days later, when she falls asleep chatting with me late at night on the sofa—I can't help it. I snap a photo of her splayed red hair and the patch of drool spreading on the sofa cushion. Her parted lips and her smooth, peaceful face.

And I send it to Theo.

"What the fuck." He calls me back in two seconds flat.

"Hey, man." I dig the heel of my palm into my eye, already regretting this. "Thought you'd gone AWOL."

Theo scoffs, the sound crackling down the line. "Not when you're messing with Florence. What the hell, Adrian? Why is she there?"

I roll my eyes, pushing off the sofa and pacing into the kitchen.

I put water on to boil, fishing a clean mug out of the cupboard. Anything to keep my hands busy.

"Maybe because you gave us both keys, jackass."

"Well I didn't think either of you would go for it—"

"Too bad." I toss a spoon on the counter with a clatter. "It's your own fault we're here."

He steadies his breathing. I can hear him doing it—drawing unnaturally slow breaths and holding them before gusting them out.

"I don't mind that you're there. The invitation was real. I just… both of you? Is that a good idea?"

I scowl at my mug. "What did you think would happen if we both came here?"

"Well. That one of you would back down."

"Because we can't exist in the same space?"

"*Yes.*" His answer makes me blink. "You hate each other, remember? Neither of you ever shut up about it."

I watch the sleeping form on the sofa through the space above the breakfast bar. Her shoulders rise and fall, her little puffed breaths so quiet.

"I don't hate her."

Theo snorts. "Sure you don't. Well, she hates you. You're so hard on her, man. You don't give her a break."

"Someone needs to be hard on her," I say, uneasy. "Life's not all sunshine and galas. You all treat her like she's wrapped in cotton wool."

"You don't know a thing about it." I've never heard Theo like this. Low and dangerous, like if he were here, he'd actually square up to me. Never mind that I'm six inches taller. "Florence is—she's under a lot of pressure."

"She's never mentioned anything."

63

"Of course she hasn't!" I can practically see him, raking his hands through his hair. Tugging at the strands, like I'm so damn annoying that he could tear it out.

Panic starts to swirl in my gut. Gnaws at my insides.

I can't lose Theo. He's the only family I have.

"Why would she confide in you? You're very clear about how much you hate her."

My hand shakes as I reach for my mug. It's some shitty herbal tea, two steps above pond water, but I blow on the surface and take a sip. It scalds my tongue.

"I don't hate her," I say again at last. When my tight throat eases off enough to speak.

His voice is acid. "There's only one bed."

"I'm sleeping on the sofa."

He sighs, his relief gusting down the phone. "Don't hurt my sister," is all he says after that. *What about me?* I want to ask, but I can't do it. It's too needy, too desperate. And he and I both know the deal—when it comes to me and Florence, Theo will pick his sister. Always.

That's the difference. He's all the family I have. And I don't count compared to his blood.

Theo starts to chatter, relaxed and nice all of a sudden, but I'm not doing it.

"Bye, man." I hang up without another word, tossing the phone on the counter. He'll get over it. Unlike his sister, Theo doesn't hold grudges. And he's the one who put me in this foul mood. I drum my fingers on the breakfast bar, peering into my mug of pond water, then curse and tip it down the sink.

A shower. That's what I need. A scalding hot shower.

And when I come out, Florence Lane can piss off back to her bed.

64

* * *

"Up." I nudge her ankle with my foot. "Come on. Time to get up."

Florence frowns in her sleep, her forehead creasing. Freckles dance across her nose.

"Up." I shake her gently, trying not to breathe in the scent of her shampoo. Theo's words echo in my ears, playing over and over in a loop ever since I hung up the phone. *She hates you.* "Jesus, Lane. Go to bed."

She makes a soft noise. A comfortable, intimate kind of noise—one that sends sparks shooting up my spine.

I ignore them and drop into a crouch. Scowl at her from eye level.

"Lane." My voice is hushed. Velvety. But when she squints open one eyelid, I glare. "Get the hell off my sofa and go back to your stolen bed."

"What time is it?" She mashes her face into the cushion, groaning like I never spoke.

"Time to piss off."

She huffs a tiny laugh. And goddamn me, I melt. A smile tugs at my mouth before I can smother it. Warmth spreads through my racing chest.

I've been sickly, jittery, since my call with Theo. Since I felt my only anchor tugging away. But the way she chuckles and sits up, blinking at me with bleary eyes, so freaking trusting...

"Come on," I say, softer this time. "You'll sleep better in the bed. And you've got work tomorrow, career girl."

She rolls her eyes, but she's smiling too. And when she scrambles up off the sofa, she takes my hand and lets me pull her.

I should let go of her hand.

I don't.

"You're nicer at night," she murmurs, tripping after me across the living room. I squeeze her palm, thinking about what Theo said.

You're so hard on her.

"I could be nice in the day." What pressures does a girl like Florence have to deal with? Too many boring financial meetings? But there's something there. Now that he's pointed it out, it's obvious. I can see it in the shadows behind her blue eyes.

She snorts. "I'll believe it when I see it."

"Challenge accepted."

She squeezes my hand back. "Don't hurt yourself, Griffith."

Theo's bedroom is shadowed. Moonlight spills through the huge glass windows, washing the double bed's white covers silver. I lead her all the way to the bedside, not ready to let go yet, and flip back the covers. I wave at the mattress, but she doesn't climb in.

"I need to change," she says quietly. "Put my pajamas on."

The thought of those skimpy satin shorts… I swallow a groan.

"Okay." Damn me, I still linger. What the hell is wrong with me tonight? "Well. Goodnight."

I drop a kiss onto her forehead before I can stop myself. She inhales sharply, blinking up at me with those big blue eyes. Then I plunge out of the bedroom back into the safety of the living room, my stomach tangling into knots.

She pauses, the only sound from the bedroom her quiet breaths. Then she crosses to the door, the floorboards creaking, and eases it shut.

My pulse slows gradually. There's a wall between us now. A

wooden door. Barriers; safety.

Not to mention her brother. My best friend.

Don't hurt my sister.

I groan and drop onto the sofa. What a night.

* * *

Jax pokes his head into the studio just as the client lets out a ragged groan.

Rib tattoos. They can look good, but they're a torture session. The guy stretched out on his side can't figure out whether he's ticklish or just in agony. I ignore them both, frowning intently at the line I'm drawing.

It's a ship and anchor. Old time sailor vibes. With seagulls spinning around the sails, and an octopus twined around the anchor's chain.

"Jesus Christ," the guy puffs. A bead of sweat slides down his temple.

"He can't help you now." Jax sidles into the studio, his boots thudding over the linoleum. "Septum piercing after this." He turns to me with a smirk. "The same girl whose belly button you did."

I grunt, laser-focused on the rib design.

"She asked for you," Jax prods. "Requested you specifically."

I finish up and sigh, rolling my neck as I straighten up.

"Guess I'm good at my job."

Jax snorts. "Sure. That's it."

Snide words crowd up my throat, but I don't spew them out. I pack up my tattoo gun, then clean up the guy's ribs. Give him the spiel about taking care of an open wound.

Jax is probably right. That's the part that stings. The septum

67

girl doesn't want my skills—she wants another chance to flirt. When I pierced her navel, she was squirming all over the bench.

It was goddamn annoying.

"Time for a break?" I've been flat out all morning. Just client after client, lining up at the door.

It's good. That's what I want—more commission. Less time until I open my own place. But my head is pounding and my throat is dry, and my shoulders are knotted to hell from stooping over the bench.

"Sure." Jax steps aside as the client leaves. "I baked again. There are cookies on the table."

Jax fancies himself a master baker. He's so sure of his skills, he tries for exotic combinations.

Ginger and cumin.

Paprika nut muffins.

My gut sinks, but I force a smile. "Great."

Jax waits until I'm slumped at the staff room table, my hands wrapped around a steaming mug of black coffee. The he drops into the chair opposite, nudging the plate of cookies toward me.

They're dark brown. With little white lumps. They seem innocent, but I've been burned before.

"Triple chocolate." Jax cackles as I chew properly, relieved. "Michaela threatened to skin me if I didn't make something boring."

"Not boring," I mumble through a mouthful. "They're good."

Jax waves an airy hand. "They're boring." His palm cracks against the table as he lunges forward. "You know what's not boring?"

The hairs rise on the back of my neck.

Jax gives off the impression of being checked out. Kind of

dozy. But he's like those rattlesnakes that watch you from half-lidded eyes.

"What?"

Jax pulls something white out of his pocket with a flourish. It drifts to rest on the table in front of me, and my stomach twists.

"A napkin?" I don't know why I'm trying to play this off. He's got me, fair and square. There's no way that's a tattoo design—it's clearly a logo.

I get wrapped up in my own world. Doodling, my thoughts elsewhere.

And now I've fucked myself over.

"Why would my best tattoo artist be designing a logo, Griffith?"

I shrug one shoulder. Open my mouth, ready to parrot some lie. But something stops me. I owe Jax, damn it. He gave me a chance; taught me everything I know.

So I tell him the truth, though it comes out kind of hoarse.

"Been thinking about starting my own shop."

Jax grunts, a half smile still fixed on his mouth. He leans back in his chair, eyes gleaming.

"Didn't think you'd admit it to me."

"Jax..."

He holds up his palms. "Relax, kid. Just wanted to see if you'd come clean."

Saying it like that—come clean—makes it sound dirty, what I'm doing. Like it's not what every other tattoo artist with their own shop has done at some point, Jax included. But I don't want to argue on this, not when his smile seems real enough.

"You'll be good," he says suddenly. Wrinkles his nose. "Too good. Don't set up too close, you hear?"

"Sure." I wasn't planning on it. The whole point of this plan is to start new. Build something bright and fresh. Something to be proud of.

"Good man." Jax's chair screeches over the linoleum, and he claps me on the shoulder as he walks past.

He pauses by my shoulder. Peers down at the napkin.

"What're those leaves in the logo?"

Heat floods my cheeks. I keep my head ducked so he can't see.

"Ivy."

"Nice." He squeezes my shoulder then lets go. "Fancy shit. Yeah, you'll be good."

I wait until the thud of his boots echoes across reception. Then I slide down in my chair, pulse galloping in my throat.

It's fine. It's fine. He didn't fire me.

And he doesn't know about the ivy anyway.

10

Florence

"If my mother saw this, she would have a heart attack."

I fold my arms over my chest, flattening myself against the dance studio wall like I could merge into the plaster. Bright spotlights shine down on beige waxed floorboards, and sparkling mirrors line the front of the studio. Smooth walnut ballet barres are fixed to the walls, and hordes of young women drape themselves over them now, stretching and yawning.

Dani, the girl who works with me most shifts, jabs me with her sharp elbow.

"That's perfect. You need a bit of *fuck you, Mom* energy."

Whatever that is, Dani has it in spades. Her wild black curls reach past her waist, and her boobs are propped up high enough to rest her chin on. Her plump pucker of a mouth is painted cherry red, and it curls into these lethal little smirks.

God, she's gorgeous. I want to be her when I grow up.

I tell her so too, but she smacks my arm. Even in a good mood, Dani is always on the verge of violence. Over the last two weeks working at the front desk, she's covered my sides in well-meaning bruises.

"Get off, you vicious imp." I wave her away with a grin. Dani likes people who fight back.

"Don't talk about yourself like that." She points at me, her sharp fingernail jabbing close to my nose. "You're grown. You're gorgeous. You're Florence Freaking Lane."

I don't feel like Florence Freaking Lane. When I caved and agreed to come to burlesque class, I was riding high on a flawless work day. Perfectly answered phones. Happy dancers everywhere.

Now I peer around the tiny svelte bodies draped over the barre. What the hell was I thinking? I tug my sweatshirt lower, wishing it covered more of my ass.

Cindy pokes her head through the studio doorway, scanning the crowd until she sees us. She nods, taps her hand against the door frame, and walks away.

Cindy never leaves. That's one thing I've learned. The woman is a non stop working machine.

Another person I want to grow into. I'd better get on with it.

"You can try out these moves on that tattoo guy." Dani runs her palms up her sides as she sways her hips, like she's picturing Adrian's hands, and jealousy tightens my throat. "If you don't want him, I will."

I made the mistake of pointing Adrian out when he walked past the lobby one morning. Dani wolf whistled, cursing loud enough for him to hear on the sidewalk.

"I want him," I rasp. I don't even know if that's true—all I know is the thought of Dani with Adrian makes me want to set things on fire.

"Say no more." Dani takes her hands away. Twines a curl around her knuckle. "He's yours."

Okay. I know you can't claim ownership over people. I know

that, but a primal satisfaction still twists my mouth.

Adrian is *mine*.

I test the thought out. Spin it around in my mind, checking it out from all angles. Try to imagine what that would be like.

He's hated me for years, sure. But lately, the ice has thawed. And that one night, a week or so ago, when he kissed me on the forehead...

Well. Maybe he was briefly insane. He certainly hasn't repeated it since, no matter how many times I make my forehead available.

The door slams against the wall—never mind that it was already propped open—and a woman in her early forties strides into the studio. She's striking, with olive skin and glossy brown hair piled on her head, a regal tilt to her chin, and dark eyelashes that sweep her cheeks each time she blinks.

"Ladies." Her voice is throaty. Low. I bite my lip, nerves buzzing under my skin, as she smirks around the room, meeting our eyes one by one. Her gaze lingers on me—on my baggy sweatshirt, my crossed arms. Her smile widens.

"Let's begin."

* * *

"Oh my god." Fifty minutes later, I sprawl back against the wall, the cool surface heavenly on my flushed skin. The sweatshirt lasted approximately twenty seconds into class, before the teacher clapped her hands and told us all to strip down to our base layers.

In my tank top and leggings, I'm exposed. Every swell of my body, every generous curve—it's all out there for the world to see. And the dance moves make it worse, with their thrusting hips and the way we slide teasing hands up our waists, just like Dani did earlier.

It's funny, though. For once, I don't feel fat. Or I do, but not in a bad way.

I *am* fat. It's right there in the mirror.

But I also feel so damn sexy.

"Get it, girl!" Dani hops towards me, raising her hand for a high five. I grin at her, sweaty and exhausted. "Mother Lane is turning in her grave right now."

"She's not dead."

Dani shrugs. "Potato, pot-ah-to."

She's ridiculous. She makes no freaking sense, but I can't help creasing into giggles. We lean against the wall together, watching another group of girls dance through the routine.

"This feels like it should be illegal," I whisper. "Like drugs or something."

"Hell no." Dani jiggles her chest. "This is as healthy as eating your veggies." Her smile turns sly. "Try it out on tattoo guy."

"Adrian," I murmur absently. "His name is Adrian."

It's ridiculous. Right? Even if Adrian and I were—were *something*—he wouldn't want to see me like this.

Probably.

The guy won't even sit too close to me on the sofa. There's no way he'd want me dancing all over him. Even if the thought of straddling his strong thighs, pushing him back until his face tips up to mine—even if it makes me flush redder than ever before.

Dani snorts. "Yeah. You're gonna do it."

I chew on my thumb nail as I scoop up my bag.

Maybe I won't give him a striptease. But there is something I can do for my new roomie.

* * *

"Fuck fuckity fuck." I snatch my hand back with a hiss, a red welt shining on the side of my wrist. Steam billows toward the kitchen ceiling, three pots spitting and simmering on the hob. I shove my wrist in my mouth, darting to the sink and running a stream of icy cold water.

"Ow. Ow ow ow. God, this is the worst." The welt darkens as I tilt my hand under the spray, the surrounding skin going chalky pale. Adrian's laptop chatters away from the counter, the cooking tutorial progressing with merciless speed, and I sniff sadly at the steam-filled air.

At least it smells good.

"Alright." I smack the faucet off. "You've got this. You're Florence Freaking Lane."

There's a strangled cough by the door.

"Oh, no." I point a wooden spoon at Adrian's grinning face. He's late back again. Where the hell does he go after work? "Don't give me shit for this, Griffith. I'm doing a good deed."

I lean over the laptop, winding the video back to the part where I scalded my wrist. The pair of disembodied hands on the screen ladle another spoonful of broth into the risotto.

"A good deed, huh?" Adrian wanders into the kitchen behind me, his socked feet padding quietly over the tiles. Honestly, even if he levitated, I'd know where he was. I'm weirdly attuned to him. Like some kind of tragic tuning fork. "Yeah, no, I get it. The world needs more half-burned risotto."

"Don't be a jerk." I steal a glance, but he's teasing. The corner of his mouth tugs up into that lopsided smile. Adrian comes close, really close, leaning one hand on the counter as he watches the video over my shoulder. His warm breath drifts over my cheeks.

My traitorous heart somersaults in my chest.

Damn it.

"I'm sweaty," I warn him, flapping a hand at him without looking. Acting more casual than I feel.

"That's nice. Thanks for the update."

"I took a dance class."

"Oh yeah?" He's half listening. Squinting down at the comment section, with despair for humanity brewing in his eyes.

"Burlesque." I don't know why I blurt it out. He probably doesn't even know what it is. But Adrian straightens suddenly, chin tilted down to me. Watching me with an unreadable expression.

"Burlesque? Like stripping?"

"Yeah. Kind of. Artsy stripping." I shrug, my heart climbing into my throat. He's so freaking close, I'm breathing in his scent. Adrian smells like soap and basil and the faint tang of fresh sweat. "What's wrong with that?"

His eyes rake down my body. I fight the urge to tug the hem of my tank top. I should have put my sweatshirt back on; should have changed into something looser when I got back after class. But I was all fired up to cook, to hunt down another win, and now—

"There's nothing wrong with that." His voice is low. Barely a murmur. "Will you show me what you learned?"

I snort. It's cartoonish—a loud, strangled hiccup of a snort, but he doesn't grin and back off. He presses a fraction closer, crowding me against the worktop.

"How's the cooking going?" Adrian traces a knuckle down my bare arm, not even looking at the hob. He's too fixated on the trail he's drawing on my skin; the way goosebumps erupt in his wake.

"It's okay," I rasp. "There should be enough for both of us. I mean, if you want some. I know we don't really cook for each other, and whatever you made would probably be nicer—"

Adrian slides one hand into my hair, my messy topknot wobbling to one side. He ducks his head, bringing his lips slowly closer until they hover a hair's breadth above mine.

Then nothing. I stare up at him, wide-eyed, like a rabbit in headlights, until I realize: he's giving me a chance to say no. To push him off and walk away.

As if.

I grab two fistfuls of his t-shirt and tug him down.

Adrian groans as his mouth meets mine. The sound reverberates through his chest under my hands; it rattles all the way down to my bones.

He sounds like he wants this as much as I do.

Even—impossibly—more.

Adrian flattens me fully against the kitchen counter, his body flush against mine from head to toe. I have to crane my neck to reach his mouth, he's so tall, and his broad shoulders block out most of the electric light. Kissing him is like being wrapped up inside him—in his arms, his scent, his taste.

He draws my bottom lip between his teeth and bites gently.

Holy shit.

"You are sweaty," he murmurs when he moves away from my mouth, kissing along the underside of my jaw.

I swat his shoulder. "Shut up. Don't ruin it."

"Yes, ma'am."

The risotto hisses behind me, the steam billowing into the kitchen turning acrid. The smell of burning tickles my nose.

I don't care. Neither does Adrian. The whole apartment building could burn down around us and I'd still stand here, kissing him in the ashes. He reaches around me, leaning toward the oven, and I grumble, but he just flicks the heat off.

"Don't want to burn your masterpiece." He buries both hands in my hair, scratching gently at my scalp as he kisses me again. His tongue nudges past my lips, and I suck in a sharp breath, spine bowing against him.

"Not a masterpiece." I speak the words against his mouth.

He shrugs, shoulders shifting under his soft black t-shirt.

"Disagree."

I tug him closer. Closer. There's no way he can get close enough. Not here, not crowded against the kitchen counter. Not with all these clothes in the way.

"Adrian—"

A key slides into the lock. We both turn, confused, then leap apart as the door swings open.

"Honeys, I'm home!" Theo sings, striding into the apartment. His luggage bag is slung over one shoulder, and a pair of sunglasses are perched on his red hair. He's wearing dark pants, a crisp white shirt and a burgundy blazer. My brother looks expensive.

He brightens when he sees us, flushed and frozen in the kitchen. "There you are." He snorts, dropping his bag on the living room rug. "I can't believe you're both alive. I thought for sure one of you would go down for murder."

I force a laugh. "Right. Hi, Theo." I sneak a glance at Adrian, but he won't meet my eye. He's too busy staring at my brother as he strolls across the living room, chattering away about his travels—blissfully ignorant to how we were just defiling his kitchen.

"I'm glad you're both here, actually. I've missed you. You can both stay, but you'll have to fight over the sofa."

Adrian's jaw clenches. A muscle leaps in his temple.

Look at me, I will him. I just want him to look at me. Even a tiny, awkward smile would do the trick.

"I'll sleep on the floor," Adrian mutters. Then he strides out of the kitchen, dodging around Theo as my brother wrinkles his nose over the hob.

"Oh, God. Florence. What the hell have you done?"

I scrub a hand down my throat, watching Adrian's back disappear through the doorway. "Risotto."

Theo chokes out a laugh, flicking the wooden spoon.

"Good effort. So, uh. Pizza?"

11

Adrian

"Florence Hyacinth Lane!"

I snort from my seat on the balcony, sketching a client's design on a notepad. I've never heard her middle name before, and definitely not in Theo's strangled yell.

My pencil whispers over the paper, shading sections. Embellishing. This may be my day off, but I have two more designs to work on after this.

I'm slammed. The knowledge that I'm taking advantage here, that I'm relying on Theo's hospitality—it sets my teeth on edge. It seemed like such a great plan when I figured the apartment would be empty, but now that it's crowded with three of us...

I need to move on.

So I've been taking extra appointments. Working overtime. Charging for more elaborate designs, trickier tattoos. Jax has raised his eyebrow a couple of times, but he doesn't interfere.

It's kind of a relief, now that he knows.

I'm not sneaking around. Not screwing anybody.

Just trying to make my own way.

Theo shouts for his sister again, the sound bouncing around the apartment, and Florence yells back from inside the bathroom. The sound of the shower drumming on the floor drifts through the closed door, but apparently Theo's too pissed off to wait.

"Florence!" He pounds on the door. "They cut me off. They fucking cut me off!"

I slide down an inch in my chair, frowning at my sketchpad. This is none of my business.

It was only a matter of time. Surely they knew that? Their mother called two days ago and accused Theo of 'harboring a fugitive'. Florence gnawed on her bottom lip through the whole call, clearly terrified that her brother would cave and kick her out.

He didn't. Despite his dramatics, Theo's not like that.

"Jesus Christ." He collapses into the other balcony chair twenty minutes later. "What a mess."

"You said you were going to get a job," I point out evenly.

Theo snorts, flicking at my eraser. "I don't know why I came to you for sympathy."

I say nothing. He knows what I think about this stuff. I've been prodding him to get a career since he graduated college.

He always agrees. Says he wants that. But then he freaks out, overwhelmed by the enormity of the real world, all the crap you have to wade through just to function every day, and he finds a new way to put it off for a month.

Like a sudden trip to Amsterdam.

"What are you going to do?"

He sighs, cracking his neck. "I already called about a job in the city yesterday. It's a tech company I interned for in second year. They're interested."

Even in this, Theo walks through life blessed. He shifts in his chair, suddenly awkward. He knows it.

"That's good."

He smiles at me, relieved. "Yeah. About time, anyway."

"Theo?" Florence hovers in the doorway. Her red hair is damp from the shower, her towel slung across her shoulders, and her feet are bare below her leggings.

She sounds so nervous. Tremulous and sad.

I swallow and look out over the roof tops.

"Hey, Flo."

She blows out a breath and pads onto the balcony. I don't look, but I can feel her moving. Can feel her warmth just out of reach. I close my eyes and focus on the sunshine instead—the spring warmth which washes over our table and tickles the potted plants.

"Do you want me to go?" She asks it quietly. It's a fair question, one I wondered myself.

After all, what's keeping her from going back there? Boredom?

Kind of selfish to strain her brother like this.

"No. Of course not." Theo sounds firm. Protective. I tense in my chair, straining to hear every whisper.

"I don't want to cause you trouble. I could go back for a little while, just until I can save enough to rent somewhere of my own—"

"No. It's not good for you there."

I'm dying here. If they don't spell it out for me, I'm going to explode. But when I squint open an eye, peering at Theo, he gives me a quick smile and changes the subject.

"You should have seen the guys in Amsterdam, Flo. You'd have died on the spot."

82

Damn it. I scrub my hands over my face, like I can wipe away the blatant curiosity written there.

Okay, I get why Florence wouldn't tell me at first. We were circling each other like spitting alley cats. But since we kissed that night...

I thought something might have changed.

"What are you working on?" Her soft voice interrupts my brooding. But I'm still too bitter, tangled up in knots, and my answer comes out harsh.

"A design for a client."

She waits for me to say more.

I scowl down at the table.

Why am I like this with her? With both of them? Theo is the brother I wish I had, and Florence—she's something else. Something so bright and golden, I can't look directly at it.

But every time we nudge towards something good, something great, desperate energy crackles under my skin. Makes me lash out and drive them away.

"You won't get anything out of him." Theo sounds knowing, and it makes my teeth clench. "Adrian's being mysterious. He thinks it makes him sexy."

I roll my eyes, but Florence breathes a soft laugh.

"It does a bit."

Holy shit.

I jerk my chin up and find Theo watching me, eyes narrowed. His gaze flicks between us, and his caution is clear.

Theo does not want me anywhere near his baby sister.

I force a smile. "All the ladies like jerks. It's scientific fact."

They start bickering then about what women want, about what gay men want, about the idiocy of straight men everywhere. I tune it out, gathering up my stuff.

83

It's nice out here, but too crowded with the three of us. I duck back inside.

* * *

The email comes in on my lunch break. Well—if you can call scarfing down a sandwich at 3pm between clients 'lunch', anyway. I lean forward, the front desk chair creaking ominously, frowning at the computer screen.

It's an invitation.

Addressed to me. Not Jax. Not Rocksteady. Me.

For the biggest tattoo convention in the country.

I swallow my bite of sandwich, mouth suddenly dry. Brushing the crumbs off my jeans, I click open the email, scanning the text with my pulse thrumming in my ears.

Last minute opening… A place in the showcase… Opportunities for premium appointments… Industry judges…

"Want a coffee?" Jax yells from the staff room. I jump, dropping the rest of my sandwich onto the lino.

"No, thanks!"

My cheeks flush as I clean up quickly, tossing my food in the trash. I forward the email to my personal account, palms sweating like a criminal. This must be how the Lanes feel every day. Like their emotions are broadcast right there on their faces.

"What's up with you?" Jax shuffles into the lobby, bringing me a coffee anyway. He thumps the mug down on the desk, leaning over to read the screen.

I click onto the booking schedule, lightning fast.

"Nothing." He grunts, straightening up. "The guy with the rib piece canceled his follow up."

Jax cackles, nudging my mug towards me with hairy knuckles.

"He's gonna walk around with half a tattoo on him? Not likely. Not for long. Just wait until he gets the first woman home and she asks to have a look at it."

I hum, lifting the coffee to my lips. It's lukewarm already, tangy from the cheap instant granules.

"You gonna call him?" Jax pushes. He might laugh, but he hates leaving jobs half done. But what am I supposed to do, chase the guy down the street?

"I sent an email. He's probably just sore. It'll heal over and he'll get brave again."

"Like childbirth."

I snort. "If you say so."

The front door swings open, a young couple squeezing through the gap and shaking the spring raindrops from their hair. They're giggling and whispering to each other, holding hands as they browse the posters on the walls, and maybe it should be cute, but all I can think is *please, don't get each other's names*.

"Listen." Jax speaks quietly, leaning in like the couple might eavesdrop. Like they give a shit what we're muttering about by the desk. "I've got a guy coming in later."

I wait, but he doesn't elaborate.

"Okay… for an appointment?"

"To interview. Since you're moving on, you know."

Ah. That explains the shifty way his eyes keep moving. The downturn to his stubbled mouth. I stare at my boss of five years, dismay clogging my throat.

Moving on.

I'm not ready. I haven't saved enough. Shit.

I nod, exhaling when Jax takes the hint and gets off the desk. Shuffles back to the staff room. Then I snatch up a scrap of paper, scribbling some quick numbers in the corner.

All that overtime.

The deposit back from my landlord.

The extra commissions.

The money saved from not paying rent.

I strain to remember it all—every sum that's dropped into my bank account over the last month. I've been scrimping like a maniac, cutting costs to the bone. Walking an hour to work each way every day. Buying groceries on offer and stashing them like a doomsday prepper.

The email floats across my mind. That convention... the ticket price is insane. It would wipe out all the progress I've made.

But if I could make enough of a splash—if I could make a name for myself—I could charge higher. Set myself up for years.

I groan, sitting back in the chair, ignoring the curious looks from the whispering couple. The answer is there right in front of me, but still, my gut tangles in knots. I'm already leaning on Theo. If I mess this up...

How long will his patience last?

"Shit." The girl titters nervously in the corner. I snatch up my mug, taking a horrible gulp. "Shit."

12

Florence

"Look! Oh my god. Look at this." I bound up to Adrian as soon as he walks through the door, his shoulders slumped with fatigue. He blinks down at the scrap of paper I'm waving in his face, a line creasing his forehead, but when he catches my wrist and gets a look at it, his expression softens.

"Congratulations, working girl," he says quietly.

"Baby's first paycheck!" Theo whoops from the kitchen. I roll my eyes, but I clutch the paper tight to my chest like it might float away.

I did it.

All by myself. No family connections, no greased palms—nothing.

Just my own hard work.

"Feels pretty good, huh?" Adrian kicks off his boots, shrugging his jacket off to hang on the peg. I open my mouth to ask him where he goes every night after work, why he gets home over an hour after I do, but Theo strides into the living room with a bottle of gin held high.

We step further apart automatically, though we weren't even that close. It's a reflex. Ever since we kissed that one night, we've been dancing around each other in choreographed politeness. If Theo thinks it's weird, he hasn't mentioned it—he's probably too relieved that we're not bickering.

In the rare moments that we're alone, when Theo runs out to the shops or shuts himself in his bedroom to make a call, we're... different. Not relaxed, exactly, but not tense and guilty either.

Like we're both waiting for our cue.

"I start work tomorrow. Flo's been paid. And Adrian is..." Theo twists his mouth, gazing at his best friend. "Well, he's as mysterious and gorgeous as ever."

A surprised laugh bursts out of me, and Adrian cracks a rueful smile. Warmth spreads through my limbs, and suddenly the night stretches out in front of us, empty and breathless.

"We're celebrating," Theo declares, unscrewing the cap of the bottle. "And this is the last good alcohol we'll afford for ages, so you dipshits had better appreciate it."

"You got mixer?" Adrian steps around us, moving to the kitchen. I watch him go, his muscles shifting under his gray cotton t-shirt.

"Down, girl," Theo mutters. "The poor man isn't a slab of meat."

"You're such a hypocrite!" I slap his shoulder with my paycheck. "Remember in your senior year, when we spent the day at the lake—"

I break off as Adrian strides back out of the kitchen, three glasses and a bottle of tonic in his hands. His eyes flick between us, but he says nothing. Just walks past and nudges the balcony door open.

"That was different," Theo says quietly. "It was puberty. I was held hostage by my hormones."

"Well, my hormones are still going strong."

"That's disgusting." Theo bumps me with his hip on the way past. "Get it together."

I can't tell if he's joking. Theo's like this sometimes, his humor so dry that you can think that you're messing around and having fun, then he turns around and eviscerates you. I follow the guys out to the balcony slowly, pausing by Adrian's hoodie draped over the arm of the sofa.

Before Theo came back, I wore it all the time. I didn't even think about it. My hand hovers over the fabric, my thoughts churning, when a cool breeze gusts in through the open doorway. I shiver.

Screw it. I pluck the hoodie up and shrug it on, cheeks burning.

It's just a piece of clothing. It's not a big deal.

* * *

We stop after one drink. Not enough to get tipsy, but enough to make us spread out in our chairs and laugh a little louder. Theo's the one who snatches the bottle away, thumping it on the balcony floor beneath the table.

"Alright, that's enough. I have work tomorrow, you animals."

Adrian says nothing, like usual, but his mouth crooks as he looks at his best friend.

"It's too bad you're going in the other direction," I put in, reaching over to flick a leaf clinging to the railing. "We could have driven in together."

"Or I could have clung to the back of Adrian's bike."

89

The air changes. Goes stiff and heavy somehow, like there are unspoken words clogging the space between us. My stomach flutters, even as I blink around, confused. But the moment passes, and Adrian asks Theo something about his new job.

Weird.

I burrow deeper into my stolen hoodie. The soft fabric reaches my fingertips and grazes the underside of my chin. It smells like Adrian, manly and clean and delicious, and I suck in big sneaky lungfuls of him while they chat.

Theo raised an eyebrow when he saw me wearing it. But Adrian—he hid a smile, his eyes crinkling.

So there.

The balcony is lit by moonlight and the city lights. Endless glowing squares, with little shadows moving inside, all wrapped up in their own lives as much as we are. I mention that to the others, and Theo scoffs, but not in a mean way.

"You're philosophical when you drink."

"I had one glass! And it was weak, you stinge."

He shrugs, unapologetic. "We're rationing. Like wartime."

When Theo clatters back inside, banging pots and pans around to announce to all the neighbors that he's cooking dinner, I expect Adrian to follow. That's always how it was with the three of us: Theo and Adrian, thick as thieves, and me tagging along behind.

I never realized they minded until that bust up at Theo's leaving party. The sudden memory of that night, with Adrian's snarled insults and cold derision—it makes me quiet. I curl up smaller in my chair.

"You okay?"

He always reads me. Sometimes I wish he wouldn't.

I nod, my chin brushing my folded knees. "Yeah. Just

90

thinking about old times."

Adrian goes quiet then too. Like he's watching the same movie reel, played out over the stars.

"Florence—"

"We'd better get back in." I push my chair back and stand. Brush my hand over the table, before I remember I left all my crap inside.

"Lane."

I skirt around him, heading for the door. His hand shoots out and wraps around my wrist, his grip gentle but firm.

"Florence. Wait a moment."

The problem is, I don't think I can. Remembering him the way he was that night, angry and rigid, it's like a bucket of ice water down my spine. I want to go back inside to the warmth, to Theo's hapless cooking and sharp teasing. To the golden electric light and the soft heat rising up through the building.

"Wait," he murmurs again. And like an idiot, I do. I stand there, aimless and awkward, as Adrian pushes to his feet and moves behind me. He nudges me forward, his chest at my back, until we're stood by the railing together, gazing out at the rooftops.

"Tell me." He places my hand on the metal bar. Wraps his own around it, until we're gripping the bar together, ivy tickling our wrists. His presence is a solid wall of heat at my back, and I sigh and melt against him. I'm only human.

"I'm just being morbid."

His mouth hovers by my ear. "Go on."

"I was…" His lips graze up my throat. "I was thinking about that night. Theo's leaving party."

Adrian's lips pull away, and cold night air swirls in to take their place. I gnaw on my bottom lip, waiting for his harsh

91

words. His dismissal. Anything.

"I'm sorry. About what I said—all of it." His chest nudges closer. Flattens us together. And I breath a sigh, tipping my head back to rest on his collarbone.

"It doesn't matter now."

"It does if it bothers you."

I shrug, his hoodie bunching. "It doesn't usually. But I don't want…" I pause to gather my thoughts. To get this right. "I don't want to be unwanted anymore. Following after people who wish I weren't there. Not that *you* have to want me," I add quickly. "You and Theo have done loads for me. And I'm really grateful—"

"We always want you," he interrupts. His lips drop back to my throat, tracing a line up to my fluttering pulse point. "*I* always want you."

I grip the railing tighter. I can't tell if I'm in danger of toppling over to the street below or floating up to the muted stars.

"Adrian…"

He listens carefully, but I don't know what else to say. So I take his free hand, gather my courage, and place it on my waist. He squeezes me there, exploring and massaging, and I choke back a laugh before I tug his hoodie and my tank top up.

His warm, dry palm meets my bare skin. He stills behind me, then presses closer.

This is what we do: urge each other closer, closer, closer.

"I'm—I've got curves," I babble inanely. Like I'm warning him of danger or something ridiculous.

Adrian hums appreciatively and strokes tiny circles with his thumb.

"You're gorgeous, Lane."

"And you don't have an ounce of fat on you. Just muscle."

92

"Does it matter?" he asks idly, smoothing his palm around to the center of my stomach. He dips his pinkie into my belly button. "I never thought you'd body shame me, Florence."

"Shut up!"

He chuckles and nips at my earlobe. Heat floods my whole body—a simmering hot tidal wave crashing right through to my core. I stifle a moan, swaying back against him as Adrian explores my bare skin, taking a leisurely tour of my hips, my waist, the sensitive underside of my breasts.

"No bra." He nudges the back of my head with his nose.

"Why should I?" I splutter. "I'm at home."

"Hey, I approve." His hand skates higher, higher, cupping me there. Squeezing gently. Grazing my nipple with his thumb. Every nerve under my skin is tingling. Heightened and ready, practically vibrating for his touch.

A clatter from the kitchen makes me jump. Adrian sighs, presses one last kiss to my neck, then pulls his hand out from under my clothes. Theo's strangled yells float out to the balcony, and cold air washes over me as Adrian steps back.

"I'd better rescue him." His face is calm in the moonlight when I turn, but his eyes gleam bright. "Are you okay?"

My cheeks ache, I grin so wide.

"Yeah. I'm okay."

Once his footsteps echo across the living, I slump over the railing, light-headed. Something swells in my chest until I can barely breathe, and I count glowing city windows until I can trust myself enough to go back inside.

* * *

"What's got you so blissed out?"

Dani clicks her tongue as I cross to the front desk, my satchel slung over my chest. I nearly ran late this morning, I was so busy mooning over Adrian. Picturing him in the shower. Daydreaming about him over breakfast.

"Gross." Dani flicks a stapler over. "It's tattoo guy, isn't it? You're all sexed up."

"I'm not sexed up." I drop my bag with a thump and kick it under the front desk. The dance studio is quiet this early, filled with bright morning sunshine, and the smell of fresh coffee floats in from another room.

In ten minutes, we'll prop the doors open and streams of wafer-thin ballerinas will flow in from the street. They'll chatter among themselves, way too perky for the morning, their buns scraped back so tight that my eyes water in sympathy.

I peer through the glass windows, but there's no sign of Adrian on the street. He leaves so early, I don't even see him in the mornings.

Workaholic.

"Do you think he'll give you some ink?"

Her question takes me off guard. I frown down at the desk as I set the stapler back upright.

Would Adrian give me a tattoo? Probably. Honestly, the option had never even crossed my mind. If I ever dared mark myself like that, my mom would freak—

"I'm gonna do it." The words are out before my thoughts can catch up. Dani whoops, barging me with her pointy shoulder.

"Hell yeah! Get my name on your ass."

"Shut up. I'm really going to do it."

"I believe you." She smiles, slow and wicked. "Though there are easier ways to get that man's hands on you."

My stomach prickles where Adrian touched me last night.

Where he squeezes and stroked and teased.

Dani whistles. "You just lit up like a lighthouse. Are you holding out on me?"

"Not really." I wet my lip. "He just touched me. And, um. Kissed my neck."

"*Nice.*" I whip my head around, but she's not being sarcastic. Dani leans one elbow against the front desk, leery appreciation splashed over her face. "I bet he knows what he's doing."

I don't want to think about that. I definitely have no finesse.

"I bet he's big, too."

"Please stop talking." We bicker until Cindy pokes her head in, perusing us quickly before vanishing again. I clear my throat and go to prop open the front door.

"Don't be weird about this," I plead as the first dancers trail inside. Dani clicks onto the class schedule, her lips twisted in a smirk.

"Of course I won't." She bats her huge eyelashes at me. "I'll leave that to you."

13

Adrian

I throw a t-shirt and a pair of balled up socks into my duffel where it sags open on the coffee table. I've been living out of this bag for six weeks now. Six weeks of sleeping on the bed, then the sofa, then the floor. Six weeks of being uprooted.

A weight has settled heavy in my limbs—a bone-deep tiredness that I don't think even a whole weekend in a king sized bed could solve.

"Send us photos!" Theo calls from the kitchen, his voice bouncing around the living room. In all the years I've known him, Theo has never mastered volume control.

"It's just going to be booths. Crowds. A convention center," I tell him when he pads into the living room, a steaming mug clutched in his hands. He blows on his drink, watching me pack. "Nothing worth taking photos of."

"Shut up." He sounds just like his sister. "It's going to be awesome. You'll be famous, and then I can quit my job again."

I straighten up, glaring at him, but he's laughing. His shoulders shake as he huffs into his mug.

"Not funny."

"It is a bit." A line creases Theo's forehead. He has the same milky white complexion as Florence; the same smattering of freckles and shocking blue eyes. "Are you ready?"

He doesn't mean the packing.

"Not a helpful question."

"You are, man. You'll be great."

The key sliding into the lock makes us both turn. Florence spills through the door, flushed and bright-eyed, for once not the first person home.

"Burlesque?" I ask. Theo shoots me a look.

"Yep." She drops her satchel onto the floor, rubbing her shoulder with a groan. The way her head tips back, her lips parting as her eyes flutter—

I cough. Turn back to my bag.

"What's going on?" Florence moves beside me. I don't look but I can feel her warmth, can sense her presence moving the air. Her voice drops to a hush. "Are you leaving?"

"No." I shouldn't be so goddamn pleased at her sad tone. It doesn't necessarily mean she'd miss me. Maybe she just likes my food. "I've got a tattoo convention. In Vegas. For three days."

I don't mention the eye-watering ticket price. That this is my last ditch attempt to start my own studio. That Jax has already found my replacement.

I don't want to bother them with this stuff.

"Adrian's going to be famous." Theo sips from his mug, but it's me she looks at.

"You told Theo?"

And not me. That's what she means. I told her brother and not me. And she's right, that's weird, but I don't have a good reason. I bought the convention ticket a week ago.

97

I shrug one shoulder, something squirming in my gut.

"It's not a big deal."

She goes quiet, then. And I know for sure—it is a big deal. I've messed up.

"Florence," I begin, but she brushes past me.

"I'm going to take a shower."

Theo watches her go, his eyes canny above his mug.

"Don't say it," I warn him, bending to snatch another shirt off the pile on the sofa. I don't even know what I'm warning him away from, only that if he pushes me now, I'll say something I'll regret.

I've said enough stupid things to the Lanes. A whole lifetime's worth.

"No worries, man." Theo sips his drink, eyes fixed on me, then smirks. "I won't say a word."

* * *

The apartment is quieter once Theo goes to bed. It always is. He's a ball of frenetic energy, moving from room to room with the volume dialed up high. By the time his bedroom door clicks shut behind him, the silence echoes through the living room.

"Right. Well, goodnight." Florence lays out her blanket and pillow on the sofa, her back pointedly turned. I stare at the spot on the rug where I've been sleeping every night, my joints already aching in anticipation.

"Lane." She keeps fussing, her back turned. There's one side table lamp on, and that's it. The rest of the room is in shadow. "Lane, look at me."

Florence huffs. Throws her armful of blankets down and turns.

"What, Griffith?"

I take a step forward. "You haven't called me that in a while."

"You haven't been a dick for a while." Her words are harsh, but her eyes are shining. She's hurt.

Shit.

"I'm going to miss you." I don't have a good reason for not telling her about the convention. Don't have a real excuse for being so cagey all the time. So I settle on the next best thing—the truth.

I already miss her. I'm already talking to her in my head like she's gone.

Florence scowls at the center of my chest. "You sure about that?"

"Definitely." I take another step but she doesn't back up. And when I rest my palms gently on her tensed shoulders, she blows out a rough breath and slumps. The tension bleeds out of her, like I've reached inside and pulled out a cork.

"Why are you so freaking secretive, anyway?"

I rub the pad of my thumb along her jaw, from her ear to her chin. Up to press gently on her bottom lip.

"I'm keeping the mystery alive."

She rolls her eyes, but there's no vitriol in it now. And when the pink tip of her tongue sneaks out to touch my thumb, I hold my breath.

"What do you want from me, Adrian?"

She sounds so wary. So tired. And I hate that; I hate that she's afraid of me on some level.

"I want to make you feel good." Her eyes widen, but I keep talking. "I want to give you something to remember me by."

Her smile is lopsided. "You'll only be gone for three days." She falters. "Um. Right?"

"That's right." I rest my other hand on her hip. Rub my thumb back and forth. "Three days and counting."

It's the easiest thing in the world to kiss her. To duck my head and seal our mouths together. After all this clumsy, awkward circling of each other, when I finally do it, it's like sinking into a warm bath.

"Adrian." She clings to me with shaking fingers. Plays with the hair at the nape of my neck, so goddamn shy. Florence sways in my arms as I kiss her, pliant and trusting, and pressure builds in my chest until I can't stand it anymore.

"Sit down." I break away, sucking in a deep breath. "Lie back on the sofa, Lane."

She plays with my hair as I settle on top of her. As I kiss down her throat and chest. She idly slips the strands through her fingers, like now that she's started she can't stop, and it occurs to me that this is the most I've been touched in years. A pit of loneliness yawns wide open in my stomach.

I nudge my head against her until she scratches my scalp. Press down harder on top of her, until her softness is flush against me everywhere.

Better. But still not enough. She fidgets and sighs as I flick the button of her pajama shirt open.

"Only you would wear buttons to bed." I slide my hand inside, tracing over her flushed skin. Even in the dim light, I can see the blush spreading over her chest. And below that, a smattering of freckles.

"It's not my fault you're fashion-challenged."

I flick another button open, then cup her chest. She's heavy and warm in my palm.

"On second thought, I like it. It's like unwrapping a gift."

"You're so full of it." Her foot drags lazily up my calf. Then, abruptly, she says: "Take off your shirt. I want to see your tattoos."

I do as she asks, whipping the fabric over my head. Self-consciousness gnaws at my gut as I sit back, letting her greedy gaze roam over me, but I breathe a laugh when starts to trace the lines.

"They're beautiful."

"I didn't do these."

Florence snorts. "That's weird. I thought you were the only tattoo artist in the whole wide world."

I want to be the only one in *her* whole world, but I manage to keep that to myself. It's bad enough that I'm so jealous of her attention, her regard for someone else's design.

"I'd do yours," I blurt. "If you wanted one. I mean, I don't have to." I'm babbling now, heat climbing my neck. "You might not even like them. Or worse, you might be a wimp."

"I do want one, actually."

Her answers knocks me off kilter. My hand pauses, partway down her stomach. Since when does little rich girl Florence Hyacinth Lane want a tattoo?

"Please don't get a guy's name," I manage.

"Not even yours?"

I jerk back, startled, but she's smirking. And as she holds my gaze, she flicks the last three buttons open. Her pajama shirt pools on either side of her ribs, the smooth expanse of her skin ghostly in the moonlight.

I dart a quick glance at Theo's door.

His bedroom is silent.

"We'll be quiet," Florence murmurs. Like she can sense my sudden hesitation. "Or we can stop here. Either is fine."

No. No way. I didn't bumble my way through six awkward

weeks of longing to falter here, with her spread out beneath me. I dip my head and lick a stripe up her belly, stifling a laugh as she gasps and squirms.

"Too late now, Lane. Unless you tell me to stop, I'm going to lick you like you're my last meal."

That blush glows brighter. My heart slams harder in response. I hook my fingers in her waistband, waiting for her nod to drag her skimpy little shorts down.

"You've been teasing me." I drop them on the floor in a puddle of satin. "Driving me insane while your brother is right there."

She shrugs. Tries to play it off. But her voice is strangled when she says, "It's a small apartment."

"So it is." I nip at her hip bone. "Better keep it down."

Her thighs are soft on either side of my head. This is the essence of Florence: softness and warmth; wicked gasps and shaking sighs. I screw my eyes shut as I lick her so I can hear her better. So I can absorb every detail and commit it to memory.

When I slide two fingers inside her, rubbing at her walls, she bows up off the sofa. Her breaths come faster, her hands leaving my hair to scrabble at the cushions for purchase.

So this is what victory feels like. I've had my ass kicked by life for so long, I wasn't sure I'd ever feel it. But feeling Florence Lane buck up against my hand, seeing her clap a hand over her mouth to stifle her moans—

I've won. Savage pleasure floods me, filling me to the brim.

"Give it to me," I growl against her core. "Stop holding back. I want to feel you come on my tongue."

Her shaky sigh is the best thing I've ever heard. And I lick her as her body tenses, as her muscles shudder, as wave after wave crashes through her frame. I work her until she slumps boneless against the sofa cushions, her cheeks bright pink and her blue eyes shining.

I sit up and wipe my chin. She reaches for me, groggy yet determined, but I slip out of reach, pushing to stand beside the coffee table.

"I have an early bus." I drop a kiss on her forehead.

This moment is perfect. I don't want to muddle it.

"Get some sleep, Lane." She mumbles goodnight, sliding her pajamas back on with clumsy fingers. I crouch in front of her and do up her buttons, then kiss her again. I can't resist.

My heart doesn't stop pounding for another hour at least. And I lie there on the rug, staring out at the blurred city lights.

14

Adrian

I fucking hate crowds. The noisy press of bodies, the muggy heat, being clipped by stranger's elbows. Random people stepping on the back of your heels, pushing at your shoulders like they have a right to touch you.

I jerk my arm, shaking off a strange hand.

Goddamn it. Why am I here again?

Because it's your last chance.

The convention center is cavernous. There are more floors than I can count, endless rumbling elevators. An indoor city of booths. When I first got here two days ago and set up, a headache squeezing my temples, a whisper of despair slid through me.

How can anyone hope to stand out here? I'll be lucky if I don't wander down the wrong corridor and get lost forever. But this is it, my last gamble, so I shoved those doubts deep inside and focus on trying not to scare people away from my booth.

Resting bitch face. That's what Theo says I have. At least a tattoo convention is filled with scary motherfuckers.

"You got appointments left?" A biker looms over my booth, his craggy eyes frowning down at my designs.

"No. Sorry." He grunts, unsurprised, and I give him a card instead. My new logo winks up at him: Ink & Ivy Designs.

I try not to think about what will happen if I don't get my own studio after giving out these cards. How humiliating that would be.

But hey—I booked out. My slots all went before lunch on the first day yesterday, and my head's been spinning ever since.

They're a premium rate. More than I've ever charged at Rocksteady. And the crowds here snapped them up like hot cakes. At first, I figured it must be a mob effect. That all the artists must be booked up too.

But they're not. I wandered around the booths on a ten minute break yesterday. Some of them still have loads of slots left.

"Can you squeeze in a little one?" A woman leans over my table, her hip jutting out. Chestnut curls tumble over one shoulder. She plays with her hair, winding it around her finger, and I open and close my mouth.

"Uh. No, sorry. I'm all booked up." She pouts but takes my card. Static fills my head as she wanders away—guilt and panic swirling up my thoughts.

I don't want her. Her flirting set my teeth on edge.

But shit, I miss Florence.

For the millionth time since getting on the bus to Vegas, I wonder what she's doing. Whether Theo's giving her a hard time. If her job is going well.

If she misses me too.

I push that thought away, standing and rolling my neck. I've got an appointment in five minutes, and I need a clear head.

But more than that, I'm straying into dangerous territory. The Lanes have always cared about me, but they've always been fascinated by me too.

I'm like an exotic pet.

One they could get bored of at any time.

"Ready, man?" My client beams from the other side of the table. It's a young guy, so young I had to check his ID, and he's bouncing on his toes with excitement.

It's contagious, and I find myself cracking a smile.

"Sure. Come on through."

He hurries around the table, making a beeline to the station I've got set up against the wall. Some of the artists put the bed right at the front of their booths, putting on a show for the crowds like those sushi chefs who cook at your table.

I'm not there yet. And besides—a tattoo is a private thing. It's intimate.

"I'm so freaking nervous." The guy tugs his t-shirt over his head and sits on the bed, his thin chest heaving.

"Don't be." I snap on my glove. "It's gonna look good as hell."

* * *

By the end of the second day, I'm so tired my vision is fuzzy. I groan, standing in my empty booth, and dig the heels of my palms into my eyes. All around me, the convention center is emptying out, the crowds snaking slowly to the exits, their steps slow as they compare fresh, raw designs and make plans for drinks and food.

I'm not going drinking. Hell—if I went to a restaurant, I think I'd fall asleep on my plate.

I snag a tragic-looking sandwich and a packet of chips from

a vending machine on the way up to my hotel room and call it good.

The place I'm staying is a dive. It had to be, after the gut-punch of the ticket price, but that doesn't stop my shoulders from sagging when I push through the hotel room door.

The carpets are bald. An ancient rug only half-covers a huge stain. And there are water marks climbing the walls.

It doesn't matter. I trudge to the bed, to where I've spread my sleeping bag over the covers. I don't trust these sheets, and anyway—it's freaking cold in here. The AC is permanently jammed on full blast.

"Jesus Christ." I mutter to myself as I toss my sad dinner down. I should be happy. No, I should be *thrilled*—I've made more in the last two days than I have in the last two months. But instead of triumph, all I'm feeling is tired.

"Don't do it," I tell myself, but I'm already dialing. Pressing the phone to my ear.

"Adrian?" Her voice hits me square in the chest. I suck in a shaky breath, my eyes squeezing shut.

"Hey, Lane."

"What's up? Are you trying to get hold of Theo?"

And just like that, I split open down the middle. How cold have I been to her over the years, if she still thinks I don't want to be around her? If it's so unthinkable that it's her voice I need to hear after a long day; her smile I'm desperately trying to picture?

"No." I cough once. "It's you I'm after."

"Oh." Her surprised pleasure warms me up. I sit carefully on the edge of the bed, tearing the sandwich packet open with one hand. "Um. That's nice. How's the convention going?"

"Good." She waits, but that's all I've got, never mind that I'm the one who called her. And honestly, how do they even let me out in public? I search for something else to add, but my tongue is stuck to the roof of my mouth.

"Good." Florence huffs a tiny laugh. She doesn't sound mad, or freaked out that I've called her with nothing to say. And that more than anything makes my shoulders relax.

"I'm not good at phone calls."

"No?"

"But I wanted to hear your voice."

She hums, pleased. "That's nice," she says again, sounding surer now. "I wanted to hear yours too. I actually—"

She breaks off, and I can practically hear the blush flooding her cheeks.

"What?" My cheeks ache from smiling. "Tell me, Lane."

"I can't."

"Why not?"

"It's embarrassing."

"Even better." I scrub a hand over my jaw as she scoffs. But then her voice drops, going quiet. Hesitant.

"I thought... you know. Maybe you were calling to talk to me."

I frown at the peeling wallpaper. "We *are* talking."

"No, you know." She sounds strained. "*Talk* to me, talk to me."

"Oh." Heat floods beneath my skin, warming my aching joints. I sit up straighter, the sandwich forgotten beside me. "Florence Hyacinth Lane. Are you talking about phone sex?"

"Shut up."

My smile fades as something builds in my chest. Something urgent.

"Right. Are you alone?"

"Yes," she whispers. "Theo's in his bedroom."

Jesus Christ.

"Go into the bathroom and lock the door." I hear the distant creak of the sofa as she stands. The hurried pad of her footsteps across the living room floorboards. I can imagine it all—the glow of lamplight. The stars winking through the glass.

"Okay." She's breathless as the door clicks shut. The muffled thump of the bathroom lock clangs through my exhausted brain. "I'm, um. I'm here."

"Stand in front of the counter. Look at yourself in the mirror. Are you there?"

"I'm there."

I screw my eyes shut tight, trying to picture it exactly. Her cute little pajamas, her wild red hair. That blush spreading down her throat.

"Tell me what you see."

"I'm, um." She's speaking in a half whisper, and it's like she's here, murmuring in my ear. I run a hand down my throat as she says, "I'm wearing your hoodie. I wanted to smell you. Is that weird?"

"Not weird," I manage, voice tight. "What else?"

"I'm, um. My hair is damp from the shower. I went to burlesque earlier. And—"

"Tell me about burlesque."

She falters. "It's a dance. I don't…"

"I bet you look fucking amazing." She waits for me to keep talking, her breath held. "I'd give anything to see you dance, Florence. For you to dance for me, somewhere private, and take your clothes off piece by piece."

"I could do that," she rasps.

"I know you could." My voice gets lower, rougher, and I sit

forward, resting my elbow on my knees. "You're so fucking gorgeous, Lane. I'd cut off my arm to touch you right now, but I'm not there. You'll have to do it for me."

I don't know where these words are coming from, so confident, so sure, but I don't care. My headache fades into the back of my skull and I focus on this, as intently as when I'm inking a design.

"Yeah?" It comes out like a squeak. "H-how?"

"Slide your hand under my hoodie. Like I did on the balcony. Do you remember how I touched you?"

"Uh-huh."

"Do it now. Feel how soft you are. How perfect." She hums, fabric whispering down the phone, and I squeeze it so hard that it creaks. "Now trail your hand up to your chest. Slowly. And when you get there, pinch your nipple, hard."

She groans, shameless and guttural, and I curse as I press down on my swollen cock. I don't want any distractions, not yet—I need to hear every hitched breath, every shaky exhale.

"I'm wet." Her whisper takes me off guard, and my thoughts scatter like leaves blown in the wind. "I'm already so wet and achy. I can feel it without even touching."

"Good," I grind out. "That's good, sweetheart. But you should touch yourself there to be sure."

"I already did earlier." Her voice is still hushed, but I can hear her confidence growing. Probably because she can hear my ragged breaths, the way she's giving me a fucking heart attack. "In the shower. I—I made myself come thinking about the night before you left. Imagining it was your hands on me. You inside me."

"Jesus." This is getting away from me. Up until now, it's been me in control. Winding her up and making her moan. But

Florence has knocked me sideways, has ripped the situation out of my grasp and turned it back on me. I palm my cock again, heart thundering. "You want me to fuck you, sweetheart?"

"Uh-huh. And I—I want to taste you. Like you did for me."

This can't be real. I feel like a tool as I pinch my forearm, but the sharp sting of pain confirms it. This isn't some exhaustion-fueled fever dream, Florence Lane is really saying these words to me, and I'm staring at the hotel room wall, too tongue-tied to respond.

"You can taste me," I finally rasp. "You can suck my cock, sweetheart. I bet your mouth is so hot and so perfect that I'll forget my own name."

She moans quietly, and I can hear a distant rhythmic rustle. She's touching herself. Getting off. Panic nips at my insides—God, what if I mess this up—but I gather every scrap of focus and force myself to keep talking.

"I've wanted you for so fucking long. Remember that weekend when we went to the lake with Theo? All I wanted to do was drag you out of sight, pull your bikini to the side, and bury myself in your pussy."

She stutters, her hand rustling faster. "S-someone might have caught us."

"Yeah." I press down on my cock hard enough to hurt. *Not now.* "I wouldn't have cared. I'd have kept going. You think I could stop once I was inside you, Lane?"

She moans brokenly, and I recognize the sound. The desperate tinge to it; the way she gasps for breath afterwards.

I should not be so goddamn satisfied that I know how she sounds when she comes.

"Oh my god." A long moment later, she's mumbling. Tired and slurring. "That was—wow. Did you... are you...?"

111

"Yes," I lie. I don't want to keep her on the phone. Make her listen to me jerking off. I know it's the same, that we're in this together, but I still can't do it. What if she hears something she doesn't like? "I, uh. I came too."

"Good." I can hear her relieved smile in her voice. Then, she says something that guts me even worse than hearing her moan. "I miss you, Griffith."

I'm hollow. "I miss you too."

15

Florence

D ani whistles long and low the second I walk through the front door. I roll my eyes, but I can't hide the shy smile spreading over my face.

I still can't believe Adrian and I did that.

A crimson-painted fingernail jabs in my direction. "That's what I'm talking about. Hell fucking yeah."

"Don't say it."

"Flo got fucked!"

"Shut up. I did not."

Dani deflates, drooping over the front desk. Sharp little origami cranes are scattered over the wood—a sure sign that she's bored.

"What? Why not?"

"Adrian is—" I glance around, but the studio is empty. No one lingers within earshot on the sidewalk. "He's away. At a tattoo convention. He gets back this afternoon."

Dani perks back up, bringing up the day's schedule with a brisk flick of her wrist over the keyboard.

"Perfect. He can deflower you then."

"I do not have a *flower*—"

"Morning, girls." Cindy raises an eyebrow from the office doorway. "All set up?" She watches wryly as we jump to finishing opening the studio. For once, Dani keeps her mouth shut as I prop the front door open, buffing away a mark on the glass with the hem of my polo shirt.

"I'd like a word with you later, Florence," Cindy says suddenly. I freeze, my pulse thrumming in my throat. "Swing by my office on your break, okay?"

"Sure." The word comes out in a whisper. Cindy watches me, face unreadable, and God, have I messed this up already? "No problem."

She nods once, a brisk dip of her chin, her bun wobbling on the crown of her head, and Cindy has almost turned back to her office when a high voice floats through the front doorway.

"Florence? Oh, for goodness' sake. You're a shop girl?"

As one, all three of us turn to face the sidewalk. My mother blinks at us, her sculpted nose wrinkled and her eyes dewy with concern.

"Mom." Cindy's eyebrows shoot up her forehead, and I fight the urge to crawl under the desk in shame. "Not now. Not here. Please."

My mother walks into the studio lobby as though I never spoke. Her lips move soundlessly as she mouths the name written on the wall: Wonderland Dance House.

Her clap echoes through the silent room. "Alright. Time to go."

Seriously? I clench the edge of the desk, heat crawling over my skin.

"No. How did you find me?" Before I've finished asking the question, I already know. There's only one possible answer.

Theo.

Mom waves an airy hand. "Your brother made me promise not to do anything if he told."

"Great," I say flatly. "You're both liars, then."

"Oh, don't be so dramatic."

"Mom." I take a deep breath. "You need to leave." I throw a nervous glance at Cindy—God, why is she still standing there?—then draw myself an inch taller. "I'm at work. I can't do this here."

"Florence, don't be so rude—"

"Mom!" My shout is too loud. It echoes around the lobby, and behind my mother, two teen girls duck through the doorway, wide-eyed. They scurry to the desk, paying Dani for their class in whispers.

I steal another glance at Cindy. She's frowning, her mouth turned down.

"Let's go." I round the desk and take my mother by the elbow, marching her back onto the sidewalk. I drag her thirty feet down the street, far enough that the dancers can't hear.

Then I give it to her.

"I can't believe you did that. Do you know how rude that was? How much trouble you could get me in?" Mom huffs and tugs her arm free, smoothing the creases on her sleeve, and I grip my hair at the roots.

She's insane. My family is insane.

No wonder Adrian hated me too.

"You can't come here again."

"Don't be ridiculous—"

I interrupt, voice cold. "If you do, I'll call the police."

Mom breathes in hard through her nose, shock rippling over her delicate features. "Florence."

115

This is it. If I can't say this now, I never will. So I square my shoulders and count my points off on my fingers, one by one.

"You can't come to my work. You can't comment on my clothes. My choices are none of your business." How the hell did it take me this long to say these things? Now that they're out in the air, huge weights lift off my shoulders. "It's my life, Mom. And if you can't respect that, if you can't respect me, you can't be part of it anymore."

The silence is thick. We stand there on the sidewalk, quiet except for the cars rumbling further down the street.

Then, faintly, she says: "Fine. If that's what you want."

I slump, so freaking relieved, ready for this fight to be over. I lift my arms for a hug, to start moving past this already, but she's already walking away. The tail of her scarf flutters over her shoulder in the breeze, and she doesn't turn her head.

My mother leaves without saying goodbye.

* * *

For the last three days, all I've thought about is the moment when Adrian comes home. But now, hearing his key slide into the lock, I stay rooted in my seat on the balcony.

The showdown with my mother... the pain of watching her walk away...

I'm numb.

"Hey." He strides into view a few moments later, eyes crinkling with relief when he sees me. He looks so tired, so worn down, and for a split second it feels like this is what we have in common: being worn thin by life.

But then he smiles, and it's like when the sun rises over the rooftops. The knot loosens in my chest, and I bounce up out

116

of my chair, breathing easier than I have in hours.

"Hi." My pulse doesn't settle until I'm squashed up against his chest. Until I can breathe in his scent and squish my nose against the hard muscle.

"Where's Theo?" He peers back inside around the apartment, his chin scraping over my head, but he doesn't unwind his arms from around me. I love him for that.

"At Mom and Dad's." I untangle myself reluctantly, avoiding his eye as I let him shrug his jacket off.

"Oh yeah? They're making up?"

"I doubt it," I mutter. Theo was almost as pissed at Mom as I am at him, and I came home ready to kick his skinny ass.

"Hey." Adrian tucks a finger under my chin. Tips my face up until I meet his eye. His looks back at me, warm and concerned, and something shivers through my insides. "What's going on? Talk to me."

So I do. I tell him about Cindy's mystery summons—the chat she was too busy for in the end. I tell him about Mom turning up at my job, being so rude, making me look so bad. About her leaving me like that on the sidewalk, cool and distant, her back straight as she walked away.

Adrian listens to it all, his thumb rubbing at my jaw, and waits until I'm done speaking to ask the obvious question.

"What happened, Lane? What's this really about?"

So I tell him that too.

It's a relief, honestly. I've been skirting around this topic for weeks, dodging his questions and avoiding his eyes, but now that I'm laying it all out there, I can hear how ridiculous it is. How I should have left long before, and I'm doing the right thing now. How ashamed I am to leave it this late.

"I'm proud of you," he murmurs when I'm done, and I melt

right there on the balcony. Why the hell didn't I tell him before? He's not nearly as harsh as I think he is. And when he ducks his head, kissing me like it's as natural as breathing, I know what I want to do.

"Are you tired?" I nudge him back by the chest, walking him slowly back into the apartment. It's a stupid question, really—there are dark shadows bruising his eyes—but Adrian shakes his head, his gaze intent on me.

I steer him around carefully until the backs of his legs hit the sofa, then push.

Adrian sits with a grunt.

"You wanted to see me dance, right?"

Holy shit, I can't believe I'm doing this. The question feels so freaking dumb, but he nods quickly, his jaw clenched as he shuffles back against the cushions. There's no music, but my heart is pounding loud enough that he must surely hear it too.

"Don't make fun," I whisper, stepping back to face him across the rug. Adrian swallows, looking pained.

"I won't. I wouldn't."

"I know," I breathe, and raise one arm overhead. Jut out my hip. And begin the routine we've been learning in class.

In the lessons, we dance to loud, thumping music. But here, with only our shared breaths as a backdrop, I go slower. Smoother. Holding his gaze.

"Florence." He says my name, but barely any sound comes out. Adrian watches me move like if he blinks, I'll disappear. He's rapt, hypnotized, and heat spreads through my limbs. I toss my hair, I swing my hips wider, and he stifles a groan.

It's heady, the feeling of his gaze on me.

Powerful.

My fingers toy with the hem of my top. I'm in a soft pink

118

draping sweater, one with a loose thread on the shoulder and a tiny nail polish stain on one wrist, but from the worshipful way Adrian watches me, you'd think I was draped in silks. And when I draw the hem up, inch by teasing inch, Adrian leans forward so slowly the sofa creaks under his bulk.

"Show me," he rasps when I pause with the hem just below my bra. I hold my breath and pull the top over my head, and he hisses between his teeth. "Ah, fuck."

It's nothing new. Nothing he didn't already see that night on the sofa, but this is different. We're not wrapped in shadows in the middle of the night—buttery evening sunshine fills the apartment, and we're exposed together in the daylight. The longing on Adrian's face makes my chest ache, and he must see something similar on mine because he swallows hard, his throat bobbing as he reaches for me.

"Lane. Come here."

I half-listen. I move closer, standing between his thighs, but I keep dancing, slow and sensual. Adrian leans back to watch me better, his gaze scorching, but his fingers play at the outsides of my thighs. They trace tiny circles, absent-mindedly, like he doesn't even realize he's touching me.

"What do you think?" I murmur when I'm nearing the end of the routine. I grip his shoulder, rolling my body towards him in a wave.

"It's good," he croaks. Clears his throat. "Really good. You've always been so fucking sexy, Lane."

This is news to me, but right in this moment, I believe him. It's hard not to when there's a tattooed, sculpted god of a guy gripping the edge of the sofa so tight, his knuckles go white.

"Likewise." I ditch the routine, sliding my fingers into his hair. I scratch at his scalp and he bucks into my hand like a cat before pressing his face against my bare stomach. "Huh. That tickles."

His hot breath makes me squirm. Sets a steady throb between my legs.

"Good. It's your turn to be tortured."

He tugs me onto his lap, firm and sudden, and the air rushes out of me in one go. His mouth seals against mine, hot and demanding, like he's punishing me for teasing him so badly. Like I have that effect on him. And I cling to his shoulders, scrambling closer, closer, and grinding myself down on his lap with a moan.

"Fuck." Adrian breaks away, staring at the wall, teeth gritted. "Is Theo—"

A muffled thump outside the door answers his question. I leap up, fumbling for my shirt, and barely have time to tug it back on before my brother crashes through the door.

"That woman, I swear to God." He tosses his keys on the coffee table. "She should pay for my therapy." Theo clatters through the apartment, a whirlwind of grumpy energy, flinging his belongings around and ranting loudly about our parents.

I know what he's doing—trying to make amends. Trying to make me feel better.

I close my eyes and try to remember that I love my older brother. Even if he ratted me out to our parents; even if he cockblocks me like his life depends on it.

"What are you guys up to?" His blue eyes flick between us, narrowing with suspicion. Adrian shrugs, wordless, and if he's not going to answer, I'm not either. I stomp off to the kitchen to grab a drink.

Behind me, I hear Theo asking about the convention. Adrian answering in a low tone. I stare blindly into the refrigerator, cold air wafting over my cheeks, and will my racing heartbeat to slow.

16

Adrian

"Well." Jax pushes the cash register shut with a clang and folds his arms. "That's it." His thick forearms are stained with faded old tattoos and dusted with wiry hairs. We hover in the Rocksteady lobby, the silence stretching between us.

"So." I scrub the back of my neck. "Yeah. Thanks, man."

I've been dreaming of this day for so long. My last day employed by someone else before I set out on my own.

Now that it's finally here, it's kind of fuzzy. I'm going through the motions, dream-like, with Jax's words coming from far away.

"Right." He sniffs hard and hitches his belt. Then in a rush, he rounds the desk and jerks me into a hug. His palm claps against my back hard enough to rattle my jaw, and I grin as I hug him back.

"Go on with you." Jax steps back, a flush tinting his weathered cheeks. "You'll know where to find me." I nod and hitch my backpack higher on my shoulder, stuffed full of five year's worth of crap from the staff room, but Jax stops me before I can go.

"Wait. Shit. I forgot something."

He shuffles into the kitchen, muttering under his breath. When he comes back, he holds up a plate, a squashy green cupcake hunkered in the center.

Good luck. It's shamrock-shaped and covered in wobbly yellow writing. I swallow back a lump in my throat as I pluck the sticky mess off the plate.

"Thanks man. Uh. What flavor…?"

"Banana mint."

I hide my wince. "Awesome. Thanks, Jax."

Stepping out onto the sidewalk, I'm untethered. Loose and lost, with the whole world stretching out before me.

The papers are signed with the bank.

I visited my new studio this morning.

There's even a tiny apartment upstairs where I can live.

Everything I've been working so hard for, clawing my ways towards with bloody fingertips—it's happening. It's here.

Florence's face drifts across my mind's eye.

Another thing I can't quite believe is real.

"Come on." I mutter to myself as I set off down the sidewalk, the hour-long walk home so familiar to me now that I don't have to pay attention. My feet lead the way and I trudge the route on autopilot, thoughts spinning as I watch my boots hit the cracked stone.

"Oh, Jesus." I choke down the first bite of Jax's cupcake with effort, staring wide-eyed at the monstrosity in my hand. There's a trash can at the edge of the sidewalk, but I don't veer closer and throw it away.

Not yet.

It was nice of him. I don't get gifts often. And besides—it's not heavy. Just sticky. And I have miles ahead of me, with my hands free and the evening sun licking my neck.

I spin the cupcake between my fingers, reading the writing over and over, and make my last walk home.

* * *

"You're back!"

Florence is on me before the apartment door has even closed. She launches her arms around my neck, her hair flying behind her—a whirlwind of softness and floral scent. I catch her, thumping back against the wood.

"*Oof*. Hi to you, too." I grin as she nuzzles the underside of my jaw. Have I ever been welcomed home like this? Have I ever had someone waiting for me, so goddamn excited to see me?

I tip her face back and kiss her beaming mouth.

"Hi," she murmurs against my lips.

"Hi."

Theo must be out. There's no way she'd be this unrestrained otherwise, and sure enough—

"Theo went out for groceries. He says he's cooking tonight."

"Cool." I wait for her to pull back. To wander back into the apartment, or maybe to grab my hand and tug me out to the balcony. But Florence keeps snuggling closer, pressing kisses onto my throat, and heat coasts through me, tensing my frame. "Florence…"

"Uh-huh?" She unwinds her arms from my neck as she nibbles my collarbone. Runs her flat palms down my chest, my stomach, all the way until her fingers latch onto the button of my jeans.

124

She pauses there. I swallow hard, mouth dry.

Do it. I blink up at the ceiling. I want her to touch me so badly, my chest aches, but I don't know how to ask that. How to just *take* things when they're offered, the way other people seem to know how to do.

"Is this okay?" She flicks the button open. I nod, my chin scraping over her soft red hair.

"Yes. Shit, yes." Her laugh is so fucking sweet. My zipper scrapes down, so painfully slowly, and she pauses again before reaching inside.

"Huh," she murmurs as her fingers close around my cock. "Dani was right."

"Who? Wait, what?"

"Doesn't matter." She nips my chin and drags her hand up my length. All the air leaves me, and I slump back against the door. "I've been thinking about this for ages," she confesses.

"Yeah?" I grip her waist, rubbing small circles with my thumbs. Try to force myself to think straight. "Like all day?" Her hand on me—it's so good.

Florence snorts. "More like for years."

It's so honest. So sweet and open and vulnerable, and shit, I've been holding so much back. It's not fair and it's not right, and I feel about three inches tall, but I'm not strong enough to stop her now that she's started. Her grip is light on me, teasing and perfect, and every last thought in my head is zeroed in on the places she's touching me.

I'll tell her things once we're done. I'll confess to her, the way she does to me. Private, terrifying things that make my stomach flip.

"Shit." My forehead drops to hers.

"Such a sweet talker."

I grin. "Sorry."

Maybe I should be embarrassed, but it's hard to feel too self-conscious when Florence Lane looks at me like this: like I'm some kind of hero. Like she's just as thrilled by this as I am. She hooks a spare finger in my waistband, tugging me away from the door, and leads me slowly to the sofa.

"Your turn." Her shove is playful. I topple back onto the cushions, then scramble to sit up straight. I raise my hips as she works my jeans and underwear down, her hand still moving, moving, moving.

It's hypnotic. Little waves of pleasure washing over me. And when she shuffles closer, her knees on the rug, and licks her lips—

"Fuck." I cradle her cheek. "You're going to kill me, Lane."

Her spine straightens, and she smirks at me, so cocky. I love that—these flashes of her fighting spirit. How did I ever think she was a pushover?

"That's the plan, Griffith."

But what a way to go.

The first touch of her mouth sends sparks crackling up my spine. It's warm and wet and overwhelming—and when her hand grips me tighter, I stare wide-eyed at the ceiling. My fingers play in the soft strands of her hair as I will my crashing heartbeat to slow, my racing thoughts to calm down, as I urge myself not to make a fucking fool of myself.

She doesn't make it easy, though. Florence swallows me down like she's making a point, like she's stating her case in an argument. And she's right, she's winning, because her mouth is fucking heaven and I can't stop my hips from twitching up, nudging my cock deeper.

It's wrong. It's ungrateful of me, but she doesn't mind—no,

she moans and takes the challenge, shuffling closer.

"Shit. Sweetheart. You feel—you feel—"

She hums, and it vibrates right through to my bones. Florence slides a hand along my thigh, searching blindly for me until she finds my fingers grasping at the sofa cushion. She plucks my hand off, places it on the back of her head, and pushes down.

Message received.

"Yeah? You want me rougher, sweetheart?"

A messy nod. I buck up harder. She splutters a little, and my heart seizes in my chest, but she keeps going. Keeps moaning, nudging me on too. Heat roars through me, urgent and wild, and I launch to my feet, looming over her from above. Her pupils blow wide as she looks up at me, still bobbing her head, her hand still working.

"You like that?" I thrust, hitting the back of her throat.

Florence moans, her hand delving between her legs to rub at the seam of her shorts. I stare, wide-eyed as she touches herself, as her cheeks hollow, as her hair bunches in my tight grip.

I don't hear the key slide into the lock. Don't see the door open. Don't notice Theo at all until I hear his yell.

"What the *fuck*."

We scramble apart, me tugging at my jeans while Florence falls back on her heels. She scrubs her arm over her mouth, her eyes wide and horrified, blinking up at her big brother.

My best friend.

He stares at me, white-faced from fury. With loathing in his eyes. A lump rises in my throat and I try to say something, to say anything, but my mouth won't work.

He turns away.

Theo's face softens when he looks down at Florence. "Are you alright?" He crosses to her, crouching beside her, and tucks a lock of her hair behind her ear.

Florence smacks his hand away. "Of course I'm alright. He's not—Adrian wasn't *hurting* me—"

Theo pushes to his feet and crosses his arms. Florence scrambles up after him, flushed and avoiding my eye.

He wasn't hurting me.

Is that what Theo thinks? My best friend thinks I would do that. Hurt his baby sister. I scrub a hand down my face, ears ringing.

"He's using you," Theo tells her, his voice cold. "Come on, Flo. Be smart about this."

"He's not using me. Don't be an asshole."

She doesn't sound sure.

Theo scoffs, the sound grating over my skin. "What else is this supposed to be? He's hated you for years."

I find my voice then. "I don't hate her. I've never hated her."

Florence blinks at me, so hopeful, but I don't say anything more. I don't know how. Not with the room spinning the way it is, and with Theo standing here, his chest heaving and his eyes hard.

Not with everything falling apart.

"He used to ask me to keep you away from him." Theo flings the words at her, like if they hit hard enough, she'll listen. "He didn't want to spend five minutes with you, Flo."

It's not true.

It's not true.

Not for the reasons he thinks, anyway.

"Please," I rasp at Florence. But her face has shuttered. She's not hopeful anymore.

128

"Get out." Theo twitches his head towards me. "Just… get out."

I've never stayed where I'm not wanted. Not once in my life. And I won't start now.

17

Florence

The front door clicking shut jerks me back to life. I round on my brother, smacking his arm.

"What the hell was that?" I go to charge after Adrian, but Theo steps in my way, hands raised. All his bravado left the room with his best friend, and now my brother is pleading. Desperate.

"Flo, listen. I'm just trying to protect you. I know how much you loved him growing up, how badly you pined after him." I huff and try to push past him but he darts in the way. "I'm not going to let him hurt my baby sister!"

"Not a baby," I growl between my teeth. "Twenty-two freaking years old."

"Okay. But—"

"No buts." I stop trying to shove past him. Rub my temples and catch my breath. Then lay it out, as calm as I can. "I'm an adult. So is Adrian. If we want to do this—even if it's a mistake—we can. It's our business."

"He's my friend!"

I throw my hands up. "And now he's mine too! If—if he

130

wants to be. We'll just have to freaking share." Adrian's words to me from forever ago float across my mind. "It'll be character building."

My steps are clumsy as I rush out into the hall. As I pound down endless flights of steps. But when I launch through the basement doors into the parking lot, I can't see him anywhere. There's no flash of dark blond hair, no sign of his bike.

"Where…"

"There." Theo puffs to a halt at my side, squinting as he points down the street. To the man striding down the sidewalk, a groaning backpack and a duffel bag slung over his shoulder. I curse and take off running, my stupid brother jogging after.

"Adrian!" He stiffens when he hears me, but he keeps walking. Asshole. I yell louder. "I know you can hear me, you jerk."

That does it. He slows, his face a calm mask when he turns. Adrian's eyes flick between us as we jog to catch up.

"Come back," I wheeze as soon as we're level. "Theo's just an idiot."

"No, I'm—" I punch his arm. Theo curses, but looks at Adrian. "Fine. I'm an idiot. Just—come back."

"I'm good." Adrian looks anything but good. His eyes are exhausted, his shoulders tense, and he looks like he aged a decade somewhere in the stairwell.

"It doesn't matter about our—our thing." My hand twitches toward him. "You need to come home."

He frowns at me. "It's not my home."

Screw that.

"Yes. Yes it is. And—" I fish for more reasons "—you need your bike. You can't just strike out on foot. So. Yes. Come back."

I just want him to come inside. To eat a crappy dinner that

131

Theo or I burned. I want us to sit on the balcony and share a stingy drink from Theo's stash and laugh about this. Or at least try to forget it.

I want that dead look behind his eyes gone.

But Adrian looks at me with something like pity, and says, "I sold my bike. Weeks ago."

What?

All those late nights and early mornings. All those times I asked him where he went after work. Weeks and weeks' worth of this tiny, stupid lie.

What's the point of it?

My voice is shallow. "I don't understand."

But Theo does. He sighs, heavy and resigned, and says: "Yeah, that tracks. Anything else?"

And Adrian nods. "I've got my own place. A new studio. I signed the papers today."

"What?" My lips are numb. How can I know nothing about this? How can I be so horribly in the dark? I stare at Adrian, waiting for him to make sense of it, but he won't look at me.

"Congratulations." The way Theo says it, it's like an insult. "You don't need us at all anymore."

Adrian flinches, but says nothing. Doesn't try to deny it. And this time, when he turns on his heel, I let him leave. He walks away quickly, shoulders stiff, and I watch him go with a tight knot in my stomach.

"Oh." I don't know what else to say.

Theo takes my wrist, his grip gentle.

"Yeah. Oh."

* * *

132

"I'm still mad at you." I reach for the steaming mug of coffee Theo has thrust under my nose, wrapping my hands gratefully around the warm china.

Ever since Adrian walked away two hours ago, a chill has settled into my bones.

Theo scoffs, throwing up his hands as he stomps past my legs to sit beside me on the sofa. He throws himself back like he's attacking it, his wiry frame bouncing on the cushions.

"I'm sorry, okay? I'm sorry I wasn't immediately thrilled with seeing you gag on my best friend's cock."

I wince. My words come out quiet. Strained.

"Do you have to say it like that?"

His sigh gusts through the apartment. We sit in silence for a long moment, both staring around the furniture like we've never seen it before. It's too quiet in here without Adrian, too cold, too dead. He's never been loud, but we got used to him being there.

Steady and warm and sure.

"The way he looked down there..."

"I know." Theo wrinkles his nose, digging in his pocket. "I'll try calling him again."

Adrian won't pick up. I know that. Theo knows that. But we have to keep trying anyway. And every time he lets us go to voice mail, another kernel of resentment hardens in my gut.

Coward.

I have things to say to him.

"Did you know?" I blurt the question once Theo steps back inside from the balcony shaking his head. "About the studio? About the bike?"

He slumps, and for the first time I notice that Theo is exhausted too. His pale face has a gray tinge to it, and his normally gravity-defying hair has wilted.

"No." He crosses the living room and flops back down on the sofa. "No. He didn't tell me about that."

"Why?" I sound desperate, but I don't care. It's only Theo here, and he's biologically bound to love me. "Why does he keep so many freaking secrets?"

Does he not trust me?

Or does he not care enough to confide?

Theo flicks at an imaginary speck on his dark pants. "Adrian is… private. He's not like us, Flo." I open my mouth to argue, but Theo fixes me with his startling blue gaze. "He's never had a safety net. He's done everything on his own. Always."

My mouth shuts with a click. I sink back into the cushions, a horrible ache radiating through my stomach.

Adrian.

God.

For the first time since leaving my parent's mansion, a fierce longing slams into me for my mother. For her perfumed arms wrapping around me, her exasperated sighs when I say the wrong thing.

When Theo scoops his abandoned groceries off the floorboards and carries the bag through to the kitchen, I bite my lip and thumb through my phone. I know he won't pick up, I know I'm only trying to make myself feel better—

"Hey." Adrian's voice is flat in my ear. A bubble grows in my chest, so big I can hardly breathe.

"Griffith. Hi." I swallow hard, searching for the right words. And settle on: "Where are you?"

"Rocksteady." He offers it up immediately, and that's something. A breadcrumb. "Jax let me crash for the night."

"Why don't you—"

"I'm not coming back, Florence. You need to stop calling."
I screw my eyes shut tight, but it's not enough. So I draw my
legs up too, curling into a ball, digging my chin into my knees.

"We can talk about this," I whisper.

"Soon," he promises, but it sounds empty. Hollow. Like he
doesn't even believe it himself. "You'll feel better soon."

"Adrian—"

"Don't be too hard on Theo." I huff, and was that a tired
chuckle? "He's just being protective."

"Who's protecting you?" I murmur. There's a long silence,
and his voice is tight when he speaks again.

"I'll see you soon. I promise."

"But—"

"Bye, Lane."

The line goes dead. I stare at the phone gripped in my palm
under my vision swims, the glowing screen warping to the
sides.

"You got through?" Theo asks softly at my shoulder.

I sniff loudly, scrubbing at my cheeks.

Did I?

"I don't know."

18

Florence

It's weird ringing my parents' front bell. I lived in this mansion for my whole life, and this is the first time I've been here without my own key. One of the staff pulls the door open—a middle aged man whose eyebrow twitches when he sees me.

"Yes. Um, hi." I don't recognize him. He must be new, or I could chat to him. Make this less awkward. Instead, I wring the hem of my pink sweater in my hands. "Is my mother there?"

He clears his throat, remembering himself, and steps back, pulling the door wider.

"Of course. Would you care for a refreshment while you wait?"

"Better not." My forced cheer bounces off the black and white tiles. "She might chase me out with a broom."

It's a bad joke, not least because my mother wouldn't know a broom if someone smacked her with it. The man forces a polite laugh, then turns on his heel, striding to the doorway and muttering to someone there. He returns, cool but pleasant, and gestures to a bench in the lobby.

"Please. Make yourself comfortable."

Alright. I mean, I literally grew up here. I played hide and seek under that bench. But I bite my tongue and sit down like a good guest, picking a stray piece of fluff from the front of my gray leggings.

I had to talk myself down from changing before I came. From putting on something more formal, more feminine, more *Mom*.

"Florence!" I fight the urge to wince as she rounds the corner, her arms floating out ahead of her. "What a lovely surprise."

This is the Lane way. We don't talk things through. Don't acknowledge any strain. We blow up, then slam the lid back down and pretend that nothing happened. For the millionth time in the last three days, I wonder if that's why Adrian didn't tell me anything. If he has his own Griffith way.

"Hi, Mom." Seeing her again brings a fresh wave of frustration. Another line of complaints queue up on my tongue. But I swallow them back—I came to her after all. Though, hearing her heels clack on the floor, I'm struggling to remember why. "Do you, um. Do you have a minute? To catch up?"

I'm trying something new—going after what I want. And what I want is a new dynamic with my mother.

She blinks, her big dark lashes sweeping over her cheeks, then a pleased smile curls her lips.

"Of—of course! We'll go into the garden." She waves an airy hand at the staff member, and I smile at him awkwardly. "Bring us some glasses, won't you?"

"Yes, ma'am."

I drove here. I can't afford to drink, and I murmur that to her as we file back out onto the forecourt.

"With lemonade!" she calls back inside, somehow still graceful when she's hollering. She smiles at me, her hand

137

fluttering over her chest, and for the first time it occurs to me that my mother can be shy.

"So... have you had a good week?"

What an inane question. Nice one, Florence.

But Mom is a veteran socialite, and she could carry a conversation with a brick wall. "Oh, darling, you have no idea."

She launches into a ten minute epic about some landscaping they're having done near the maze. Some issue with the contractors, peppered with reassurances that the artist they're working with is "Divine, Florence. Just divine." She chatters away happily, walking briskly in her heels even over the gravel. And when we step onto the grass, she shifts her weight to her toes, floating over the grounds as easy as breathing.

I can't believe this woman gave birth to me.

"I'm taking dance classes." She splutters when I tell her about burlesque, but she chokes back whatever horrified comments she must surely have. And I'm grinning as we climb the stone steps into the gazebo—the same spot that Adrian yelled at me so many years ago.

"It's exercise, right? It's good for me."

She starts to say something, then breathes a laugh. "Yes. I suppose it is."

We sit on a bench, side by side, and gaze out across the gardens. The evening sunshine is warm, the breeze fragrant, and bees bob lazily over the flowerbeds.

In the distant, several men work by the maze, digging in an odd formation for Mom's 'divine' landscaper. One of them pauses, lifting the hem of his blue t-shirt to dab at his forehead, the shadows of his muscles clear even from the gazebo.

I slide Mom a sly look.

"How long will the workers be here?"

She shrugs, smiling sweetly. "As long as it takes."

I snort, and she titters quietly as another man in a white staff coat brings a tray with a jug and two glasses. Beads of condensation run down the glass, and the liquid inside is cloudy, clinking with ice.

"Hell yeah." I smack my lips after my first sip. It's cool and fresh, and so delicious.

"Florence," Mom chides, but there's no heat to it. And after a moment, she slumps back too with a sigh.

"I had a young man once," she says suddenly, still squinting at the workers. "Before your father. He was a gardener. Poor as anything, but such a gentleman."

I hold my breath, afraid to speak in case I put her off. She's never spoken to me like this before.

"What happened?" I urge when she trails off, taking another sip. She swallows and shrugs, lifting a manicured hand.

"Life, I suppose. But I do think of him fondly." Her sly smile returns as one of the workers calls to another. "Especially these days."

I grin, swilling the ice in my glass. Adrian's name is on the tip of my tongue—this is my chance, damn it. She's given me an opening. Whatever my mother's flaws, she's not clueless. She can tell there's something on my mind.

Sure enough: "He was rather like your Adrian."

I cough on a mouthful of lemonade.

My Adrian?

Not Theo's?

"You liked him such a lot." She smiles, wistful, and my heart sinks. She doesn't know. She's still reminiscing.

"God." I scrub at a lemonade spot on my leggings, annoyed. "You and Theo are as bad as each other. Did everyone know I was in love with him?"

She turns to me then, her pale eyes wide.

"Of course, darling. You were incredibly obvious." Mom pats my hand. "I think we were all infatuated, in our own way."

I sit back and chew that over. Mom and Dad were always kind of weird around Adrian. They hovered over him. Made awkward, loud jokes. They set his teeth on edge, it was plain to see, but I always thought they did it out of awkwardness. That they were patronizing him.

Apparently all the Lanes were soft for Adrian Griffith.

"He liked you too," she whispers, like someone might be listening in the bushes. "Theo was ever so jealous." She snorts. "Until that pool boy, anyway."

Holy shit. How much does our mother know?

I've been thinking of her as distant. Uninterested. But she's been watching us from beneath those big lashes.

"Mom." I have to say it. "I like my job."

She stiffens beside me, but slowly tips her chin. "That's wonderful, darling."

"And I'm going to get a tattoo."

Her voice is even more strained. "How marvellous. That won't at all ruin your lovely skin."

I grin wide for what feels like the first time in days and shuffle down, leaning my head on her shoulder.

"Miss you, Mom."

She sighs, winded. "Yes. I miss you too."

* * *

"He just… disappeared." I pump the cleaning spray at the mirror, scrubbing at the glass with my cloth. Dani stands beside me, her dark curls swept up by a headband, sweat beading her forehead.

It's lunchtime. This room is empty. To Cindy, that means only one thing: time to clean. But I'm grateful for the burn in my muscles, for the single-minded distraction.

At least, I was. Until Dani asked about 'tattoo guy'.

"What do you mean he disappeared? He ghosted you?"

I scrub harder. "No, not like that." I don't think so, anyway. But the more time stretches out without a word from Adrian, without replies to my texts, the less I'm sure.

He's stewing. Doing his strong silent type bit.

He'd better be, anyway. Because if he's not, if things between us really are done… I gnaw on my bottom lip, scrubbing at a smudge.

"Well, did you hook up?"

"Yes. Well, partly. Sort of."

Dani shakes her head, spritzing the mirror. "Then he didn't ghost you. It won't be that until you sleep with him."

"Thanks," I say flatly.

She shrugs and jumps to wipe the top of the glass. "I never promised to sugarcoat it."

"Girls." Cindy pokes her head in the studio. We wave our rags at her, breathing hard from the heat. She rakes her gaze over us, always taking in more than she lets on. Then: "Florence. Can I have that word?"

Shit. Dread fills me, sudden and cold. I forgot about our scheduled chat. The mysterious meeting. It can't be good, right? Not with the way Cindy's mouth presses into a firm line. I glance at Dani and she blinks back, worried.

"Be back in a second," I whisper, hoping to God that's not a lie. The studio floor echoes loudly under my steps. Cindy leads me all the way through the winding halls, shutting us in her office before she says a word.

"So." She rounds her desk. Starts sorting through piles of paperwork, like she just can't stay still. Her eyes flick up to me, then back to her work. "Little rich Florence. You still want to be here?"

"Yes." My answer comes out in a croak.

Please don't fire me.

Please don't fire me.

"You're overqualified." She's blunt. Not wasting time. "Your mother had a point."

"No." I shake my head quickly, pulse tapping in my throat. "She didn't. She doesn't. I want to be here. And she won't come back again."

"I know." Cindy cracks a small smile, and I let out a breath. I play with the hem of my Wonderland polo shirt, equal parts hope and fear. "So I have a job for you."

Um. Isn't that what I'm already doing?

"... Thank you?" I hedge, and Cindy scoffs. Shakes her head, her glasses slipping down her nose. She pushes them back up.

"Don't thank me yet. It's going to be a nightmare. I want you to plan us a gala."

Years of stilted polite conversation, quiet string music, and the clink of champagne glasses crash into me.

"A gala?" I manage. "I've never..."

"You can do it." She straightens, impatient. "Fundraising. A showcase for the dancers. All that crap. You know more about it than we do, don't you?"

"I—I guess—"

"Good." She smirks. "You still have to clean, though."

Right. Okay then.

I leave her office in a daze. A gala. A freaking gala.

For the hundredth time today, I think of Adrian. He'd tip his head back and laugh at this; he'd tease me so badly.

My chest throbs.   Enough is enough.   I straighten my shoulders and march by to the studio with my jaw set.

I'm going to clean these mirrors. Finish my shift.

Then go find my ghost.

19

Adrian

I step back, drill in hand, and study the shelves lining my new office walls. They look level, but I've messed this up once already. It's all harder than I thought it would be, doing up my new place. Nothing like the damn YouTube tutorials.

Florence's burned risotto drifts across my mind and I stifle a smile, even though there's no one here to catch it.

She was right. It's hard learning everything from scratch.

My back and shoulders ache from long days of sanding and painting and putting up furniture. It's taking me forever to do it all on my own, and for the dozenth time I consider calling the Lanes. Asking for some more pairs of hands.

No. I scrub the back of my neck, placing the drill down on a nearby table with a thud. The studio is an empty box, draped in dust sheets and strewn with paint tins and tools. It's not good enough yet. They can't see it. I want...

I want to impress her.

It's dumb. I know it is. But I've made such a mess of things, and when the idea came to me, I latched onto it with both desperate hands. Doing up the studio and the apartment above it. Making something I can be proud of, something I can offer the girl who grew up with everything.

Like I said. It's dumb.

I dig my phone out of my pocket, wincing when I see the paint splatter on the edge. I'm careful with my things, but the paint gets everywhere. It's on more of my clothes than not. So my jaw is already clenched when I thumb through my messages, checking to see if she's tried to reach me again.

Nothing. I told her to stop calling, and she listened.

My own goddamn fault.

Nerves churn in my gut, and I distract myself swigging water from a bottle and stepping back to the center of the room. This will be the lobby. With a front desk and designs on the walls, but not those cheap plastic posters of designs any idiot could do.

Art. My best work, the kind that draws in the crowds.

The work that made my name at the convention.

I haven't even opened yet, and already I'm booked up for months.

"It looks good." I jerk at her voice, sloshing water onto the dust sheets. Florence stands in the front doorway, silhouetted against the sidewalk, the pink evening sky burning bright behind her. I shake my head, like I'm dreaming, like she's some desert mirage, but when she steps inside, the floor creaks.

She's really here.

"What... how did you know where to come?"

Really? That's the first thing I say to her? There are a thousand more important things to say, and sure enough, she hesitates, her footsteps slowing. But she answers me, raising her chin in defiance.

145

"I talked to Jax. He showed me this."

Something white dangles from her hand. Something rumpled and smudged. The napkin I drew my logo on.

"Ink & Ivy Designs," she murmurs, reading the white square. "Not too many places called that."

"It reminds me of you," I blurt. She startles, but a pleased flush darkens her cheeks. Yeah, this is more like it. "The ivy. It's for you."

"Why?" she asks, trying for casual, but she's so fucking thrilled, she looks ready to float up to the ceiling. And I've been such a dick, staying away this long. Telling myself I needed things to be perfect before I could make amends. I stride to meet her, not willing to spend one more minute without my hands on her.

She shivers when I cup her face.

"Why do you think, Lane?" I kiss her gently. Softly. With all the care that I should have shown her days ago. There's no way I can make all this up to her, but if there's even a tiny chance... "Don't you know love when you see it?"

She snorts, smacking my arm, but then her fingers wind in my shirt. Tug me closer.

"You can't talk."

She's right. But she's holding me in place, gripping tight like she's afraid I'll slip away again. So I square my shoulders and say what I should have said days ago.

"I'm sorry. I don't know why... I don't know why I hid those things from you. I don't know why I make all of this so hard."

Florence bites her lip. Shifts her weight between her feet.

"Do you not trust me?"

"Of course I do." I glare at her, like somehow this is her fault. God, I'm an asshole. But she smiles, relieved. "I just... I'm not

146

used to…" I try again. "I've never…"

I trail off.

Shit.

I'm fucking this up. It feels like the most important moment of my life, and I'm fucking it up.

But Florence plucks one hand free and places it flat on my chest. Right over my racing heart.

"I guess we need practice," she murmurs, so open and hopeful, and relief surges through me. Makes my head spin.

She sways in my arms when I kiss her, bowing backwards from the force of it. But she whimpers, urging me on, her arms hitching tight around my waist, until we're plastered together. Nothing between us.

Only heat, and thrumming blood, and snatched gasps of air.

I start to walk her back, wanting to flatten her against the wall, and I only remember the wet paint at the last second.

"Shit!" I yank her back before there's a Florence-shaped print on my wall. Before I ruin her clothes, her gorgeous hair. And she blinks at me, confused, before the haze clears from her eyes and the chemical smell of wet paint reaches her nose.

She bursts into giggles, pressing against my chest, her shoulders shaking, and I grin up at the ceiling.

Shit.

That was close.

"Come upstairs." I ask before I can think it through. The unpacked boxes, the dust sheets, the wreckage that is my new apartment. It's not ready for her, it's not perfect yet—

"Yes." She grabs my hand and squeezes. "Definitely."

Well. No turning back now.

* * *

I've imagined taking Florence Lane to bed so many times, it's like a constant movie reel in my head. Not just lately, either—for years.

She's had me wrapped around her pinkie finger since we were teenagers. She just didn't know it.

In my daydreams, there's a huge bed with perfect white cotton sheets. Maybe a balcony overlooking the sea, with silk drapes fluttering in the breeze. Glasses of wine; a basket of grapes.

You know. Romantic stuff. A setting worthy of Florence.

Instead, we've got a mattress made up with bed covers on the floor and a small apartment scattered with hand tools. A lump builds in my throat—God, what was I thinking asking her up here?—but Florence peers around with a smile curling her mouth.

"I like it," she announces. "It's light. Airy." She points at a windowsill. "You could grow plants right there."

"Ivy," I croak, and she glances at me, her eyes soft around the edges. So fucking tender.

"Sure." She hooks a finger in my belt loop and tugs me towards the mattress. "That would work."

We pause at the edge. Hovering on the precipice. And even though my heart is crashing in my ribcage, chaotic and wild, our kiss is slow. Lazy.

"I've wanted this," I tell her when we break away for air. The words are dredged up from somewhere deep and private, somewhere I don't delve too often. I rest my forehead against hers and run my hands up her waist and squeeze. "For such a long time. You have no fucking idea, Lane."

"I think I might, actually." She sounds kind of strangled, and I choke out a laugh. Her hands roam over me, just as greedy,

148

mapping my waist, my stomach, my chest. A single fingertip traces the lines of my collarbone. "Damn. You're really hot."

I should not be so smug.

But it's impossible to keep the grin off my face as I duck my head, nibbling at her neck. Florence is warm and pliant, so responsive beneath me as she sighs and tilts her head.

A palm trails lower. Down my stomach, past the waistband of my jeans. Slowly, so slowly, until she runs a hand over the hard line of my cock.

I buck into her hand, helpless, teeth gritted.

Florence tightens her grip.

"You're mine. I mean, I want you to be mine."

I nudge her down to sit on the mattress, following her and pressing her back. Stretching out on top of her. I balance my weight on my palms, attention skittering between her warmth, the feel of her curves against me, and her words.

You're mine.

"I've been yours for years." I draw her bottom lip between my teeth, nipping before I soothe back into a kiss.

I like her possessive. I like her staking a claim.

I've never belonged to someone before.

Florence arches beneath me, rubbing and sighing as I kiss the breath from her lungs. Maybe I'm not good at talking, maybe I can't say it properly with words, but this is telling her too.

The scorching trail of my hands down her body, teasing her clothes out of the way.

My greedy mouth swallowing her moans.

The tremble in my fingers when I slide a hand inside her shorts, delving and finding her slick.

"Shit." She stares wide-eyed at the ceiling as I trace her clit. As I plunge deeper, up to the second knuckle inside her. Her hips buck beneath me, searching for more, and I give it. "What are the chances of Theo walking in this time?"

I bark out a laugh, withdrawing my hand to tug her shorts and panties over her hips. Florence sits up, pulling off the rest of her clothes, then yanks at my t-shirt, impatient.

"Judging by our luck so far…"

"He'll be here any minute," she finishes with a wry smile. Her eager eyes roam over the tattoos on my chest and make my skin flush hotter. "We'd better move fast."

I don't think so. I did not pine for this since I was a goddamn teenager only to rush it now. I stand, flicking my jeans button open, and watch Florence's throat bob as she swallows.

"You look at me like I'm something to eat." I kick my boots off and push my pants down.

"Maybe you are." She's teasing, but there's an edge of warning to her words. "Maybe I'll swallow you whole."

I crawl back on top of her, wordless, and suck in a sharp breath as my bare skin settles against hers.

She's so warm. So soft. Sliding silky beneath me as I kiss and suck a trail down her throat, lingering at her chest to lave her nipples. I squeeze and knead her, throat tight from the sensation overload, and when I finally drag myself away and continue my path down, she buries her hands in my hair.

"You're good at that," Florence breathes as I hover between her legs, my warm breath wafting over her clit.

"I haven't started yet."

She shrugs, the covers shifting.

"You think I don't remember?"

I lower my head, licking a slow stripe up her center. Yeah, she remembers, and I remember too, our bodies falling back immediately into what feels good. Into what comes naturally.

I rock against the mattress, idly seeking friction as I mouth at her, licking and sucking.

"Oh, fuck." Her hips jerk beneath me and I press her down, holding her in place. "Adrian. So good. So good." I hum, relishing the shivers that race through her. Teasing her entrance with one fingertip.

She bows off the mattress as I push inside her. Slow and pulsing, rubbing at her walls. And I've barely pumped in and out of her, laving her clit with my tongue, before she's coming, her whimpers piercing my heart.

"We can stop there." I wait until she's collapsed, boneless, to sit up and swipe my chin on my forearm. "We can take it slow if you like."

"Adrian." She's exasperated. But fond. "It's been nearly ten years. That's plenty slow."

I lean over and jerk a cardboard box closer to the mattress. The contents slide and clatter as I rummage through, cursing under my breath. I could have sworn they were in here—

"Got it." I hold up the condom and turn back to find Florence biting her lip as she stares at the hard length jutting towards her.

My cock twitches under her gaze.

"Get over here," she says softly. I sheath myself and prowl forward on my hands, crowding her back against the mattress. Before, when she was on her knees, she liked it rough. Domineering.

I can do that. It's like she's whispering into the dark depths of my brain.

"Florence." I notch at her entrance. Then press forward, slow but firm. It's a drawn-out slide into her heat, her legs wrapping around my waist and squeezing tight. She urges me deeper

151

with her heels, moaning and shifting beneath me, and I hiss between my teeth as I seal flush against her.

My forehead drops onto her shoulder. "Fuck."

My hips are already rolling. I can't help it. She feels too good to stay still, and she's giving those breathy little moans, squirming to meet me. Sparks of pleasure shoot up my spine, tensing my muscles, and I rock harder. Bear down on her until our skin smacks together.

"Yes," she hisses, trailing into a throaty groan. "Oh God, Adrian."

I crack a palm against her ass, then reach between us to strum her clit. Sweat beads on my forehead as I move over her, in her, pounding her writhing body into the mattress. I study her reactions, eyebrows pinched, learning what she likes and how she likes it.

And Florence keeps no secrets from me.

From the sounds she makes to the way her back arches, the way her fingernails scratch down my chest—she lays it all out in the open. How to make her breath hitch. Which angles make her see stars. The way she likes a firm touch, a hard pace, the sting of teeth.

"Oh God." Her strained voice makes my lip curl in triumph. "I'm—I'm going to—"

"Yes," I urge. "Come for me."

One more crack of my palm sends her hips bucking, her thighs locking tight as wave after wave shudders through her. Florence clenches down on my cock and the air leaves my chest, and with two more thrusts, I follow her down.

I come so hard it almost hurts. With gritted teeth, buried deep. And for the first time in my life, I feel at home.

"Well." Florence stares at the ceiling when I collapse beside her, her hair mussed and her chest heaving. Little pink marks dot her pale skin, and her eyes are so bright they're practically glowing. "That was... yeah."

"Are you trying to freak me out?" I ask mildly, tying off the condom while I catch my breath. My words are more casual than I feel. "Because I was there too, Lane. You didn't hate it."

I toss the condom in a trash can filled with DIY scraps. She chuckles, breathless.

"No. I didn't hate it." Florence rolls over to face me, pillowing her head on her arm. "We should do it again soon, though. Just to be sure."

20

Florence

T*wo weeks later*

"Oh my God. Florence. I can't believe you're doing this." Theo leans over Adrian's shoulder, grimacing as his friend swabs my wrist with antiseptic. Adrian ignores him, calm as ever, his grip gentle on my arm.

I swallow the lump in my throat and aim for blustery confidence.

"You didn't freak out when Adrian got his first tattoo."

Theo flaps a hand. "That was purely selfish. He looked hot. You are my sister, and I cannot believe Mom and Dad are letting you do this."

"They're not." I glare at him pointedly. "I didn't ask permission. Because it's no one's business."

The hint falls on deaf ears. Theo winces, backing away dramatically as the needle starts to buzz.

"Better run faster." Adrian's tone is so dry, only his words show that he's teasing. "I'm coming for you next."

"Stop flirting. Your girlfriend is right there."

Adrian rolls his eyes, but they're warm. Crinkled at the corners.

"Will it hurt?" I whisper once Theo is out of earshot. I squirm on the leather bench, my thighs sticking to the material from the hot day.

"A bit." His thumb rubs back and forth over my wrist, encased in a blue latex glove. Adrian's voice drops lower. "I thought you liked that, Lane?"

I suck in a sharp breath, glancing over his shoulder, but Theo is far away, strolling around the Ink & Ivy lobby. Everything is pristine, from the crisp white walls to the stainless steel edging the cabinets. Behind the front desk, pots of ivy line the wall, their vines tumbling towards the ground.

I brought those.

"You want to stop?" The teasing is gone from his voice. He's serious, but gentle. There's no judgement there.

I straighten my shoulders. "No. There's only one chance to be Ink & Ivy's first client, right?"

"Right." He bends his head, all business, and I hiss at the first sting of pain. The needle drags slowly along the lines he traced. It's a small design. Delicate.

A wreath of ivy leaves.

"Classy. Understated." Dani had nodded sagely when I showed her what I planned to get, the two of us crashed out on her sofa after moving me into her spare room. And it is a gorgeous design, but honestly, I also figured if it was tiny it would hurt less.

"Motherfucker," I murmur, clearly very wrong. Adrian chuckles, his hands so steady.

"Language, Lane. What would your mother say?"

"Something like, 'What a lovely permanent disfigurement.'"

Theo strolls back into the studio, his hands thrust in his suit pants pockets and his crisp white shirt open at the collar. Through the glass windows, two teenage girls slow their steps, staring at his red hair and sharp cheekbones. He nods at them, bemused.

"What are you two whispering about?" he asks, still frowning out at the sidewalk. He comes back to hover over Adrian's shoulder, nodding when he sees the half-done design.

"Secret things."

Theo glares at me. "Screw that. Don't think you two dipshits can freeze me out just because you're boning." He jabs a finger at Adrian's head, not looking away from me. "See this idiot? I was here first."

"We're not *boning*," Adrian says calmly, reaching for a white pad to dab at my wrist. "We're in a relationship."

Theo clutches his stomach. "I'm going to throw up."

They keep bickering, but Theo's eyes are sparkling, and he throws a wink in my direction. And though Adrian's expression hasn't changed, though he's laser-focused on my wrist, I can tell he's secretly pleased.

He likes when we fight over him.

I'm more than happy to oblige.

"Back off, Theo," I say cheerfully. "Or I'll tell Adrian about the guy in your office."

"What guy?" Adrian murmurs, lowering the needle again. I hiss, squirming on the bench as Theo flips me off from behind his friend's back.

"It's nothing," he says airily, picking at his thumbnail. "Just another beautiful man who's obsessed with me."

"Must be exhausting." Adrian smirks when I kick his ankle.

"It is, actually." Theo flops onto the bench by my side. He

leans over, peering at the raw skin of my wrist. The design coming to life through Adrian's clever hands. "Damn. It does look good."

"Sorry to disappoint."

"Save it for our mother."

"You two are a nightmare." Adrian dabs at a spot of blood. My stomach clenches as I watch him—his steady hands. His flexing jaw. The way his eyes flick up to me and crinkle when he catches me staring.

I don't care.

I love him. I want him to know. And though we tell each other regularly, whispering in private, I like to show him, too.

You know. Really hammer it home.

"What time are you meeting office guy?" I'm speaking to Theo, but my eyes don't leave Adrian. Slowly, so slowly I don't make him jerk, I run the toe of my sneaker up his calf.

His grip tightens on my wrist.

Theo blows out a breath and checks his watch. "Now. Shit." He launches upright. "Bye, guys. Get all your PDA out while I'm gone."

"You must have planned that," Adrian says when the front door clicks closed, muffling the sounds of the street outside.

"Nope. Just good luck." I pull my wrist back and inspect it as Adrian packs up. He's methodical with his equipment, careful and precise, and watching him sets an ache throbbing below my navel.

"This is beautiful. Thank you."

He scrubs the back of his neck, facing away. "It'll look better when it's healed."

"Griffith. I mean it. It's perfect."

He smiles at me then, over his shoulder, and he's so clearly

157

relieved. I hop down off the bench and go over to him, holding out my arm so he can clean and dress the tattoo.

"So." I watch him dabbing at my skin so gently. "Want to go upstairs and play doctor?"

His face cracks into a smile, the evening light spilling through the windows and lighting him up.

"Sure. We have to be careful of your arm, though."

I draw a cross over my chest with my other hand. "Scout's honor." He catches my unmarked wrist and presses a kiss to the pulse hammering there.

We hover for one moment, his lips against my skin. Breathless. Waiting. Then he grabs my hand and tugs me out of the studio. We crash up the stairs, loud and laughing, and I barely notice the sting in my wrist anymore.

My unmarked arm, though—that wrist is tingling. Adrian Griffith has that effect on me.

He always has.

THE END

Thanks for reading Roomies! I hope it gave you all the delicious romance feels. If you enjoyed it, please consider leaving a rating or review!

For a grumpy neighbor romance, check out The Naughty List. Read on for a quick teaser...

And for new releases, sales, and bonus content, be sure to sign up for my newsletter!

Kayla xx

Teaser: The Naughty List

I dropped the cardboard box on the parquet tiles, strands of tinsel and cracked baubles scattering over the floor.

"Crap."

I sighed and glanced around, but the lobby was empty. No friendly faces in sight. Just glowing orange lights fixed on old-fashioned wallpaper, the bank of mailboxes, and the sweeping staircase.

Fine. Okay. I'd spent all week at work untangling string lights and decking out store mannequins in Santa hats. I could do another hour.

I crouched low, my striped elf leggings straining, and swept the halo of glittery destruction into my hand. When I'd agreed to help decorate the apartment building, I'd pictured a team effort. At the very least, the landlord Mr Henson getting his burly hands dirty. But no—I'd just spent thirty minutes dragging boxes of ancient decorations up from the basement, their cardboard disintegrating in my grip.

"Motherf—"

A shard of cracked bauble sliced my thumb, a bead of glossy crimson blood welling up in the cut. I shook my hand, cursing under my breath, and glared at the sparkling mess on the tiles.

I couldn't leave it. Someone might step on it—slice their foot—and every time someone passed this stretch, they'd see this mess and think of me. A sickly feeling churned in my stomach.

I hated disappointing people.

My phone buzzed in my pocket, vibrating through my thin elf's smock against my hip. I fished it out, wincing as a spot of blood stained the fabric, and pressed it to my ear.

"Hello? Mr Henson?"

"Are you done yet, Addie?"

His gravelly old voice was even blunter over the phone. Usually, when I passed him in the halls, he at least grunted hello. But from the tone in my ear, you'd think I was the world's biggest pain in his ass, not his pro bono decorator.

"Um. No. I just started."

The sigh rattled down my speakers.

"How long will it take?"

Indignation straightened my spine, and I leveled a glare at the hallway wall.

"Much less time if you help, Mr Henson."

He cleared his throat, and when he spoke again he was all cheery bluster.

"Oh, no rush! No rush. You'll do a bang-up job."

I rolled my eyes, tipping to the side to sit down and save my burning thighs. It was always like this: Halloween, Valentine's Day, the Fourth of July. Mr Henson sniffed out my compulsive need to please like a shark scenting blood in the water. And he got me decorating and baking and—one time—collecting tips for his 'hard work'.

Please.

Each holiday, I promised myself it was the last time. I told Mr Henson too, my voice polite but firm.

But then I heard the other residents *ooh* and *ahh* over the decorations; saw Mrs Petrova steal a paper Valentine's rose

160

when she thought no one was looking.

And I melted. I couldn't help it. I was the world's biggest sucker.

"Addie Miller. You cannot be serious."

I flapped my hand at my best friend as she stopped on the bottom step of the staircase. Mira crossed her arms, leaning against the wooden banister, staring into the pile of boxes with a wrinkled nose.

"Are there rats in there? I bet there are rats."

I shushed her, turning my head so I could hear Mr Henson grumble on. Something about lifting the residents' spirits and the rent going up.

Crap. I screwed my eyes shut, letting my forehead thunk against my knees. No way could I afford another price hike; not when I went to work in stripy leggings and a hat with a bell.

"You know what, Mr Henson?" I sounded strangled. "I have to go."

"Oh? Yes, all right," he grumbled, though he seemed to be winding up for another rant. I hung up before he could get going again and tossed my phone to the floor.

"Rents are going up."

Mira hissed. "That fucker."

"Yup."

"He'd better be paying you for this."

I cringed. I was sitting on the musty tiles, bleeding and covered in ancient glitter and an elf costume. Mira growled, twitching towards me like she wanted to strangle me.

"Are you for real? *Why*, Addie? You don't even like this shit!"

I eyed the boxes of decorations doubtfully. A ceramic angel with a chipped nose squinted back at me.

"I like Christmas…"

"This isn't festive." Mira stomped down the last step onto the tiles, lashing out to kick the nearest box. "This is old, grimy and disgusting. And you're not helping, you're compulsively trying to please a man you hate."

She had me there. I sighed and gripped the banister, tugging myself to my feet.

"It's not for Mr Henson. Not really. Mrs Petrova told me the other day that this is her favorite time of year. That the holidays keep her going."

Mira hummed, a glint in her eye. "Oh, yeah? What were you doing with Mrs Petrova?"

"I was—" I cut myself off, glaring at her. Fine: I was *helping*, cleaning up her apartment while she rested her old feet. "We were hanging out."

"Uh-huh."

She wasn't buying it. Not for a second. Mira knew me better than anyone—Hell, I spent the first six months of our friendship offering to help, to watch over her laundry in the machine or water her plants, before she snapped and told me to cut it out.

I turned away, swinging my long, dark hair over my shoulder as I bent down so she wouldn't see my flaming cheeks.

Scraggly tinsel. Splotchy baubles. String lights with half the bulbs missing. I rummaged deeper, determined to find something worth winding around the banister. The scent of mildew wafted up from the box.

"I'm going to stage an intervention, you know."

I grunted.

"This isn't healthy."

I flapped a hand at her without looking.

"Shoo, naysayer. Or get your hands dirty."

I fully expected the thud of Mira's biker boots on the stairs. Instead, a pair of manicured hands plunged into the box beside mine, and I hid a smile.

"Don't take this as approval."

"I won't."

"I still think this is pathetic."

"Noted."

"I'm just—oh, fuck." Mira slowly withdrew one hand, grimacing at the sticky residue coating her palm. She shook her head, hard, like she was snapping out of a trance, and shot to her full height. "Nope. No way. Screw this six ways to Sunday. You're on your own."

I grinned, braiding frosty white tinsel around the banister as her enraged footsteps echoed along the floor above. The slam of her door echoed through the hallway, and then it was just me and the rustle of glittery plastic.

* * *

I dusted my hands off and stepped back, surveying my masterpiece. The lobby *sparkled*: glass snowflakes spun beneath the sconces on the walls, and colored lights winked from potted shrubs. A traditional wooden calendar counted down the days of December, placed on top of the mailboxes and surrounded by frosted pine cones.

There was holly. There were candles—battery powered, but still. And clutched in my hand was the final touch: a sprig of mistletoe.

I cocked my head and surveyed the lobby. I'd spread bits and pieces through the halls, but this right here was the main event. A burst of color, with pinpricks of string lights glinting like stars.

The mistletoe rustled under my fingertips. Pearly white berries nestled in the leaves, just like Mrs Petrova's favorite pair of earrings.

Where to hang a sprig of mistletoe?

The obvious place would be the entrance way, or somewhere near the mailboxes. But visions of the creepy guy on the third floor stopped me from hanging it there.

No. Better to keep this low key. The female residents would thank me.

There was Mira's door, of course, but she was the last person to need help getting kisses. She was beautiful, with her coppery shoulder-length hair and plump mouth, and she damn well knew it. But more than that, Mira did not give a crap about what anyone thought of her—least of all men.

Apparently that was powerfully erotic.

After Mira, my closest friend in the building was Mrs Petrova on the top floor. The tiny, spherical old woman was stooped with age, but her eyes were sharp and her mind was quick. She'd cackle to see mistletoe hanging from her door frame, then swat me with her broom.

Already snickering, I clutched the sprig tight and marched towards the staircase. But at the last second, my feet veered to the right, rounding the banister and plunging down the hallway. My own apartment was down here—past the reach of the sconce lights, cloaked in shadows and right next to the laundry room. Plenty of times, I startled awake in bed after midnight, woken by the clash and groan of the machines.

That dark, noisy apartment was the only reason I could afford this building.

That, and the tiny fact that my bathroom was three doors

away down the hall.

I didn't head towards my apartment. It would be tragically desperate to hang mistletoe on my own door frame.

No. I had another target in mind.

He'd hate it. He'd be so, so pissed. I knew that, and yet I couldn't help myself. I paused in front of my neighbor's door, smirking at the peephole.

If helping was my biggest addiction, messing with Lucas Murphy was a close second. He was terminally grumpy, a malevolent presence looming over the mailboxes or stalking through the halls. In all the two years we'd spent living a few feet away from each other, he'd never once smiled at me. Not even when I knocked on his door offering cookies, or took delivery of parcels for him.

He just dragged his imperious gaze from my head to my boots, then wrinkled his nose in distaste.

Ass.

Yes, Lucas Murphy could use all the romantic help he could get. I was doing him a favor. A good Christmas deed. I ran my palm up his door frame, scanning for a hook or nail to hang my little gift.

"What are you doing?"

The deep voice made me jump. I spun around, hiding the mistletoe behind my back like a guilty toddler.

"Nothing."

"Nothing?" Lucas scowled at me, his blue eyes flicking over my shoulder to check his door. "Do you always stroke strangers' doors?"

"We're hardly strangers."

The words were out of my mouth before my brain could stop them. I winced, watching the storm clouds gather on my neighbor's face, and backed up a step until my shoulder blades hit his door.

"Oh, really? Do we work together?" Lucas advanced a step, crowding me against the wood. His shoulders were deceptively broad under those shirts.

"No."

"Do we get drinks? Go to movies?"

"No. And no."

"So we're not friends. Not colleagues. Barely casual acquaintances, wouldn't you say?"

I nodded, glaring up at him with thinly disguised loathing. Man, I hated this guy. I wanted to ruffled his black hair; knock his glasses askew. I wanted to drag him into my bathroom and give him a swirlie.

"So what, Miss Miller, were you doing by my door?"

I held up the mistletoe, dangling it between us. Lucas reared back like I'd shown him a snake, eyes widening in alarm.

Ha. Vicious triumph shot through me.

"Just decorating for the holidays. Did you see the lobby?"

He cleared his throat, recovering. "I did."

"What do you think?"

"Horrendous. If I wanted to live in a grotto, I'd move to the North Pole."

Ah, Lucas. He was consistent. I rolled my eyes, my evil prank foiled, and pushed off his door. He could be an unbearable Grinch if he wanted—I'd expect nothing less. But Mrs Petrova would appreciate the mistletoe, and I still had four moldy boxes to drag back to the basement.

"Well, this has been fun and all, but I need to get going."

"Running late for Santa?"

I frowned, confused, then looked down at my stupid elf

costume, all the way to the little bells on my curly-toed boots. Shit. I opened my mouth, ready to blurt something clever, but Lucas' door closed in my face with a snap.

Asshole. Every time, every *single time*, he always got the last freaking word.

I gritted my teeth. Counted backwards from ten. Then forced out a slow breath.

Who cared if Lucas Murphy was an ass? I had decorations to finish, a shift to go to, and a bargain-bin bottle of wine to drink with Mira later.

Unlike Lucas-Loner-Murphy, I had a life to live.

* * *

The Naughty List is a steamy holiday romance with a guaranteed HEA. Contains mulled wine, embarrassing grandparents, weaponized mistletoe, and a hot nerd so tender he'll melt the frostiest of hearts.

Available now!

About the Author

Kayla Wren is a British author who writes steamy New Adult romance. She loves Reverse Harem, Enemies-to-Lovers, and Forbidden Love tropes.

Kayla writes prickly men with hearts of gold, secretly-sexy geeks, and—best of all—she's ALWAYS had a thing for the villains.

You can connect with me on:

🌐 https://www.kaylawrenauthor.com

🔗 https://www.bookbub.com/authors/kayla-wren

🔗 https://www.amazon.com/~/e/B08CL281V1

Subscribe to my newsletter:

✉ https://www.kaylawrenauthor.com/newsletter

Also by Kayla Wren

Year of the Harem Collection:
    Lords of Summer
    Autumn Tricksters
    Knights of Winter
    Spring Kings

Standalone titles:
    The Naughty List

The Office Hours trilogy:
    Extra Credit
    Bonus Study
    After Class

Printed in Great Britain
by Amazon

85909017R00100